THE ASPERN PAPERS

A Comedy of Letters

Adapted for the theatre
by
MICHAEL REDGRAVE

from the story
by
HENRY JAMES

To
FLORA ROBSON & BEATRIX LEHMAN

SAMUEL  FRENCH

LONDON

NEW YORK TORONTO SYDNEY HOLLYWOOD

ISBN 0 573 01028 5

Please see page iv for further copyright information

THE ASPERN PAPERS

First produced by Peter Daubney in association with Michael Redgrave Productions Ltd and F.E.S. Plays Ltd at the Theatre Royal, Newcastle-upon-Tyne, on the 27th July, 1959, and subsequently at the Queen's Theatre, London, on the 12th August, 1959, with the following cast of characters:

(in the order of their appearance)

Assunta, the maid	*Nancy Nevinson*
Mrs Prest, H.J.'s friend	*Pauline Jameson*
Henry Jarvis (H.J.), a Man of Letters	*Michael Redgrave*
Miss Tina, Miss Bordereau's niece	*Flora Robson*
Miss Juliana Bordereau	*Beatrix Lehmann*
Pasquale, H.J.'s manservant	*Olaf Pooley*

Directed by Michael Redgrave

Setting by Paul Mayo

Music for the song *The Green Hussars*
composed by James Bernard

SYNOPSIS OF SCENES

The action of the Play passes in the "sala" of Miss Bordereau's house in Venice

ACT I

An afternoon in the Spring of the year 1895

ACT II

Scene 1 Six weeks later. Afternoon
Scene 2 Three weeks later. Early evening
Scene 3 Later that evening

ACT III

Twelve days later. Afternoon

THE ASPERN PAPERS

ACT I

SCENE— *The "sala" of Miss Bordereau's house in Venice. An afternoon in the Spring of the year 1895.*

The room is on the first floor, some twenty feet above the canal and garden, and gives the feeling of a grand but uncomfortable waiting-room that has seen better days. We see five walls of what must be an octagonal room. The downstage wall R *contains a door. It is never used, and at the moment there are three small chairs in front of it, one of the chairs being stacked upside down on one of the others. The next wall* R, *angled towards the wall back* C, *has a large arch. Two steps lead up to a landing which connects the stairs from below, at the downstage side of the landing and out of sight, with the stairs at the upstage side of the landing which lead to the upper floors. On this landing there is a small window, barred on the outer side, which allows a look on visitors arriving at the front door, which opens on to the canal, some twenty feet below. A smaller window is in the upstage staircase wall. On the landing there is a console table and by the window a strange lever and chain which can release the bolts on the front door below. The third wall of the octagonal room faces us, and this wall contains the main feature of the room: a pair of high, heavy doors which open outwards into other rooms: Miss Bordereau's parlour and bedroom. When these doors are open we see another pair of doors, padded with faded leather or torn baize. When this second pair is opened we see what may suggest a large room: a gilt screen and a gilt-top table. These two pairs of doors are contained in a sort of porch or alcove, surmounted by an escutcheon in painted stone or plaster, heavily cobwebbed. On each side of the porch are console tables, the one* L *broken away from the wall and standing upside down. The fourth wall, up* L, *contains a bay which matches the landing in the second wall. Shuttered french windows lead on to a balcony smothered with evergreen magnolia. From this balcony, an iron stairway, out of sight at the downstage end, descends to the garden. The fifth wall, down* L, *contains a similar doorway to the first wall down* R, *but it is purely decorative, there is no door. A large iron stove, of a gothic type, stands in front of the doorway and its metal flue or chimney pierces the wall inside the doorway. The heat and smoke from the chimney have cracked and stained the plaster of the wall. A heavy, circular table stands* LC, *with small chairs above and* L *of it. (See note on p. 75.)*

When the CURTAIN *rises, the room is empty. Two nearby church bells, overlapping, chime the half hour.* ASSUNTA, *the servant, comes up the stairs from below on to the landing. She is large and heavy, probably no*

I

*more than forty, but she looks more. She wears clacking pattens and a
black shawl. Her throat is bound up with rags. When she speaks it is in
a hoarse whisper. She carries a brass tray with a plate, and a bowl
covered with muslin. She goes to the double doors up C and opens the right-
hand door. As she does so, the front door bell rings.* ASSUNTA *puts the
tray on the table* R *of the double doors, goes to the landing window, opens
it and looks out, then returns to the double doors. She carefully makes the
inner double doors fast. This must be made quite clear. She is obviously
very anxious not to allow a disturbance. She closes the door up* C, *crosses
to the open landing window and peers out.*

ASSUNTA (*calling in a hoarse voice*) Chi é?

MRS PREST (*off*) Buona sera, Assunta. I'm Mrs Prest. Do you
remember me?

(ASSUNTA, *after a moment's consideration, pulls the lever which
releases the front door. We hear the lock open and the creak of the front
door.*

ASSUNTA *exits down the stairs* R *to meet the visitors, her pattens
clacking on the stone steps*)

(*Off; her voice growing louder as she comes up the stairs*) You remember,
Assunta? I was here some years ago.

(MRS PREST *appears on the landing. She is a strikingly handsome
American in her forties, very fashionably dressed. She speaks with a pro-
nounced and charming American accent. She carries a parasol and her
handbag.*

ASSUNTA *follows her on*)

How are your dear ladies? Well, I hope?

(ASSUNTA *moves up* C)

(*She comes into the room*) I've brought along an old friend of mine
who is very anxious to meet them.

(ASSUNTA *clutches the rags around her throat*)

(*She calls*) H.J., my dear friend. Come along up.

(H.J. *is heard coming up the steps* R)

(*She notices Assunta clutching her throat and goes to her*) My dear child!
Not the "Venetian throat"? Spring in Venice can be so treacher-
ous. (*She lowers her voice sympathetically*) I am sorry. Did they get my
letter?

(ASSUNTA *looks puzzled*)

(*She speaks with some asperity. Indeed, for all her social charm to Assunta,
she is plainly not quite at ease*) My gondolier brought it. The day
before yesterday.

(ASSUNTA *nods vigorously.*

HENRY JARVIS, *known as* "H.J.", *appears on the landing. He is also an American but he is so Europeanized and so much the Anglo-phile that he imagines that people do not guess his New England up-bringing. Very few do. He is not handsome, but undeniably impressive. A certain pomposity makes him at some moments seem to be more than his age, which is forty-five, but his general appearance is younger than that and there are moments, when he is disappointed or hurt, at which he becomes disarmingly child-like. He has considerable physical and in-tellectual vitality. His movements as well as his speech are emphatic and thrusting. He can roll off long sentences sonorously and rapidly, without drawing breath. It is his favourite form of exercise. He carries his top hat, stick and gloves and is holding a visiting-card)*

(She turns to H.J.) They got the note, Harry. *(She crosses to c, removing her gloves, and turns to look at H.J.)*

(H.J., on the landing, extends the visiting-card vaguely, as if in a dream, in the direction of ASSUNTA, *who makes a slight move to take it, but his attention is absorbed by the room in which he finds himself and unthinkingly he puts the card into his waistcoat pocket)*

H.J. What a strange—what an extraordinary room! *(He puts his hat, stick and gloves on the table* R *of the double doors)*

MRS PREST *(covering up; with unnatural brightness)* I don't see anything so very extraordinary about it, it's a very nice *sala*. Or was in its day.

H.J. *(moving down* R*)* Extraordinary. For once, a place is exactly as I imagined it. Except that it is empty.

MRS PREST *(moving to* L *of H.J.)* What did you expect? The two old ladies live alone.

(H.J. takes out a large silk handkerchief and mops his brow)

Are you sure you're quite well, Harry?

(H.J. seems to come out of his trance, and, ignoring Mrs Prest's remark, addresses Assunta)

H.J. *(to Assunta)* Are the ladies at home?

(ASSUNTA looks at Mrs Prest)

MRS PREST *(as she sweeps round up* L*)* Le sognora sono a casa?

(ASSUNTA smiles doubtfully)

Please ask them if I might see them for a few minutes. *(She takes a visiting-card from her handbag, moves and hands it to Assunta)* I said in my note that I would call this afternoon.

(ASSUNTA nods)

Grazie.

ASSUNTA. Prego.

(ASSUNTA exits up c, *carefully closing the door behind her.* MRS

PREST *turns swiftly on H.J. The ensuing conversation is conducted almost in whispers, very urgently*)

MRS PREST. H.J.! (*She moves to L of him*) Sometimes you would try the patience of a saint. Now, quickly, explain what this is all about.
H.J. There is no time. (*He crosses to the stove and closes its door*) I would have told you in the gondola on our way from the station if you had met me alone. Why did you bring that foolish Contessa and her friend? (*He starts to prowl around the room*)
MRS PREST. If your train had not been late, and if the dear, kind Contessa had not offered me a lift in her gondola, I might have missed you.

(H.J. *moves to the windows up L and looks out*)

But why, in heaven's name, did you insist on dragging us all in straight here?

(H.J. *crosses to the doors up C*)

You did not even so much as say "Thank you" to the Contessa. It was not gracious.

(H.J. *listens at the doors up C*)

Now, tell me, quickly please, what are you *up to?*

(H.J. *moves hurriedly up R, and motions Mrs Prest to be silent. ASSUNTA enters up C and crosses to L of Mrs Prest*)

ASSUNTA (*shaking her head*) No. Sleeping.
MRS PREST. Sleeping! What, both of them?
ASSUNTA (*in a hoarse whisper; partly in Italian and partly in English*) No, la vecchia, Signorina Bordereau, is sleeping. L'altra, Miss Tina, in chiesa, at the church.
MRS PREST. I hope we haven't disturbed the old lady.
ASSUNTA. She never hear nothing from her room.

(H.J. *and* MRS PREST *look at each other*)

H.J. I will meet you at your hotel, Helen, a little later. You go back now with your friends. I would like to wait a few minutes.
MRS PREST. You can't imagine that the Contessa has been waiting. She said she would send her gondola back for us.
H.J. I don't know what has come over me. I seem to have been exceptionally uncouth this afternoon. (*He picks up his hat, stick and gloves*) Let me walk you back.
MRS PREST. Nothing would persuade me to try to find our way through the back streets of Venice, even at this hour. (*She turns to Assunta*) Assunta, let me know as soon as the gondola returns, will you?

(Assunta *nods, crosses above Mrs Prest and exits down the steps* R. H.J. *moves to the landing and watches Assunta go downstairs*)

I would like to sit down, Harry. I am a little fatigued.

H.J. Oh, I'm sorry. (*He takes the top stacked chair* R *and places it* RC)

(Mrs Prest *sits on the chair* RC)

(*He takes her hand and lightly kisses it*) Forgive me, Helen.

(Mrs Prest *gives him a kind but sad smile, and leans her parasol against the back of the chair*)

Mrs Prest (*cheerfully*) I don't suppose it will be long.

(H.J. *takes another chair from* R *and places it down* R *of Mrs Prest*)

How was London? Oh, by the way, did you see the Scarabellis?

(H.J., *at the mention of the name, looks swiftly at Mrs Prest and paces a few steps down* R *in agitation*)

H.J. (*pulling himself together*) Yes, I saw the Scarabellis. (*He crosses to the table* LC *and puts down his hat, stick and gloves*) It is they who, after you, are responsible for this sudden, impetuous excursion.

Mrs Prest. How am I responsible?

H.J. (*moving* C) At the Embassy the other evening, Scarabelli was talking of you to the American Consul. He said, jokingly of course, that you would make the best wife for an ambassador that anyone could wish.

Mrs Prest. Why jokingly? And why, especially, "for an ambassador"?

H.J. Please, Helen, I beg you, do not banter with me. (*He moves up* LC) I feel I am on the verge—the perilous but perhaps redeeming verge—of the most important discovery of my life.

Mrs Prest (*quietly*) Go on.

H.J. (*moving to* L *of her*) You know my ruling passion?

Mrs Prest. I think so. Though you and I might not agree as to its nature.

H.J. Jeffrey Aspern.

Mrs Prest. Ah, yes. The early American poet. You were at one time engaged on writing something about him, were you not?

H.J. (*a little stiffly*) I am editing the centenary edition of his works, which will include a full-length biography. Joseph Cumnor is to publish it two years from now.

Mrs Prest. Full-length? But you once told me very little is known about Aspern.

H.J. (*crossing above Mrs Prest to* R) Until recently, all too little. Since then, far more. Now, with your help . . .

Mrs Prest. How do I come into it?

(H.J. *sits on the chair down* R *of Mrs Prest, and pulls it slightly towards her*)

H.J. At the Embassy the other night, Scarabelli, among your many graces and virtues, listed your kindnesses. He mentioned several names. Names of people to whom you had been a bene-factress, whom you have helped out of your big, bounteous heart.

MRS PREST. Ah! You mean the Bordereau ladies.

(H.J. *nods gravely*)

Yes—let me see. I can't remember how I first heard of them. The name sounds French, of course, but I remembered I had once known a family called Bordereau who came from New Orleans. I heard that the old lady here was ill and I had a suspicion they were in want; so I came here to see if there was anything I could do.

H.J. Did you get to know them at all?

MRS PREST (*shaking her head*) I visited here only once or twice. Even then I saw only the younger one. The old lady, I under-stand, has been a complete recluse for as long as anyone can remember. She must be very old. In her youth, it seems, she was something of a wit and more than something of a beauty. Quite the toast of the town, in fact. The younger is—well—dim. But not, believe me, without a certain still pride. She made it quite clear, without saying so, that they asked no favours and desired no attention. I did not feel encouraged to call again.

H.J. How long have they lived in Venice?

MRS PREST. They may have been born here for all I know.

H.J. Have they any money?

MRS PREST. Well, as you see, not enough to throw it about. From the outside, this palazzo looks as if, at any moment, it might crumble quietly into the canal.

H.J. (*rising and crossing above Mrs Prest to the doors up* C; *in horror*) Ah, don't! Even at this moment she may have passed away quietly in her sleep and the key to the riddle of Jeffrey Aspern lost for ever. (*He begins to pace the room*)

MRS PREST. Riddle?

H.J. (*moving down* C) The secret, if you prefer the word, of what caused the sudden, dramatic change in the quality of his writing. (*He moves up* C *and turns*) It has baffled literary biographers for over half a century. Now, I believe I am on the threshold of discovery.

MRS PREST. Don't be so tantalizing, Harry. Explain yourself.

H.J. (*crossing to* LC *and turning*) Aspern's later poems are of such quivering intensity and passion, so far above his early lyrics and "native woodnotes wild" that some critics in their blind ignorance have dared to suggest that they came from another heart, another pen.

MRS PREST. But what has all this to do with these two ladies?

H.J. It is the older one I must meet.

MRS PREST. I thought Aspern died young. You're not suggesting that he knew her? (*She pauses*) She must have been a mere infant if he did.

H.J. She was a young woman. We may hesitantly assume that she was not more than twenty and not less than seventeen in the year when their stars crossed.

MRS PREST. You mean they were lovers?

H.J. When some planetary intervention parted them or when —not to put too fine a point on it—when he deserted her, he had three years gloriously to live, before he was heroically to die, defending his adopted country, shot through the heart by the invader's bullet.

MRS PREST. When did you discover all this?

H.J. (*pacing freely up and down* c) Five months ago, at a sale of an old house in Philadelphia, an extraordinary cache of documents was discovered that had been in the possession of a cousin of Aspern's. A few business letters, a brief note scribbled from the field of battle and a package of a more personal nature, to wit, a diary; extremely revealing as to character. And what was so odd is, that although the war was long since over, the diary had been heavily censored. The package containing it was not in the poet's handwriting. It had not been opened. The postmark was Venice.

MRS PREST. You mean—(*she points to the doors up* c) that she censored the diary?

H.J. We did not immediately guess as much. (*He moves down* L.) But it was at this time that we started making enquiries. We had one salient clue. The postscript to the note written on the field of battle said that should anything happen to the soldier-poet any enquiries that were necessary could be made of a Miss Bordereau, at this address.

MRS PREST. Battle, what battle?

H.J. You will never believe it! The Siege of Venice. Eighteen-hundred-and-fourteen. The old lady cannot be less than one hundred years old. She may even be one hundred and three.

MRS PREST. Impossible!

H.J. (*turning to her*) Why? Mortals have lived longer.

MRS PREST. I mean it's incredible.

H.J. (*moving up* c) When I first heard of her actual existence, it was as if I had been told that Mrs Siddons, or Queen Caroline or Lady Hamilton—the famous one, I mean—were still with us. (*He moves down* c) But I have not the slightest doubt that the old woman now lying asleep beyond those doors is Aspern's "Divine Juliana"—"The Dark Lady of the Italian Cantos".

MRS PREST. But why did you not attempt to see her at once?

H.J. I am coming to that. (*He crosses to the window up* L *and looks out*) Joseph Cumnor, who is not only my publisher but who will share with me whatever laurels are due to those who have rescued this first truly great American poet from oblivion, wrote to her at once. (*He chuckles*) We scarcely dared hope—(*he crosses to c*) after all those years, that there would be a reply, but it was worth trying.

MRS PREST. What was the reply?

H.J. There was no reply. But we had been making enquiries. Cumnor wrote again. (*He takes his wallet from his pocket and extracts a letter*) To his second letter came a sharp answer, written by the woman we suppose to be her niece—more probably her grand-niece. (*He hands the letter to Mrs Prest and quotes it with ease from memory*) "Miss Bordereau requests me to say that she cannot imagine what you mean by troubling us. She has none of Mr Aspern's 'literary remains'." (*He moves down* L *then circles the table* LC *and goes to the window*)

MRS PREST (*reading the remainder of the letter*) "Miss Bordereau cannot imagine what you are talking about and she begs you will let her alone." What a childish hand! Well, perhaps they really haven't anything. If they deny it flat, how can you be sure?

H.J. (*moving down* C) Don't you see, Helen? They are too flat, too positive?

MRS PREST. No, I don't see.

H.J. She calls him "*Mister* Aspern".

MRS PREST. What does that imply?

H.J. It implies familiarity.

MRS PREST. Why?

H.J. You don't refer to "Mister" Shelley or "Mister" Keats, do you?

MRS PREST (*reluctantly*) It *implies*, I suppose, familiarity.

H.J. (*taking the letter and replacing it in his wallet*) And familiarity implies the possession of tangible objects.

MRS PREST. Now wait!

(H.J. *moves down* L)

Suppose I had known Shakespeare—suppose I had a lock of his hair, a button of his tunic . . .

H.J. "Doublet—doublet"!

MRS PREST. Doublet, then—would that make me call him "Mister" Shakespeare?

H.J. (*turning to face her; with considerable force*) Yes. If he had been your lover and you wished to keep the secret.

MRS PREST. But, H.J., *I* wouldn't have wanted to keep the secret. (*She considers this*) Still, I *do* see what you mean.

H.J. (*moving* C) Then you can also see why Juliana becomes for us today as potent a mystery as the Dark Lady of the Sonnets has remained for three hundred years.

(*There is a pause*)

Mrs Prest. Yes, but Shakespeare is Shakespeare, and in any case, if I remember rightly, even he seems not to have been over-anxious to have the world know who his Dark Lady was. Will the world be that much poorer if Miss Bordereau and· her "Mr Aspern" remain in the shadows which they quite obviously cherish?

H.J. (*crossing above Mrs Prest to* R *of her*) I have no reason to believe that Aspern cherished obscurity. *He* took no pains to conceal anything. On the contrary. As for her, until five months ago her secret was safe. But when we stumbled on those papers in that attic in Philadelphia, we uncovered the fragments of a genius.

(*He crosses below Mrs Prest and the table to the stove*) When Aspern disc red Italy he discovered himself. He sounded the depth of his own obliquity and he was appalled. But–he never lacked courage and he clung to that. Finally he sought expiation. The last group of poems are like burnt-offerings whose smoke still rises to the gods, long after the tide of battle has sunk without trace into the earth.

Mrs Prest (*with gentle irony*) Bravo, Harry, that was splendid!

H.J. (*crossing to the doors up* C) Who knows what treasures of his later genius are not hidden in this house? As for her—(*he moves down* C) there hovers about her name—how shall I say . . .?

Mrs Prest. An intimation of immorality?

H.J. (*wincing slightly*) A perfume of impenitent passion.

Mrs Prest. You mean he treated her badly.

H.J. (*moving down* L) Half the women of his time—to speak liberally—flung themselves at his head. While such female fury rages, accidents, some of them grave, cannot fail to occur. I judge him, perhaps more indulgently than you. It has been suggested that he was not "a woman's poet".

Mrs Prest. There seems no doubt he was Miss Bordereau's.

(Assunta *enters up the stairs* R. Mrs Prest *turns to her*)

Assunta. La sua gondola arriva adesso.

(Assunta *exits down the stairs*)

Mrs Prest (*rising and collecting her parasol*) Thank goodness! I was beginning to think that gondola had foundered somewhere.

(H.J. *reluctantly collects his hat, gloves and stick*)

H.J. (*crossing to* C) Will you come with me again tomorrow, Helen?

Mrs Prest. I shall have to consider that.

H.J. (*appalled*) Please, Helen! Without your introduction it will be impossible.

MRS PREST. Why? If a man wants something of a woman he will most likely get it, provided he wants it enough. Part of it, anyway. Sure you'd settle for part of what you want?

H.J. At this moment, I'd settle for the merest glimpse of her eyes, or the sound of her voice.

MRS PREST (*putting on her gloves*) Then think about it. There must be a dozen ways of bringing about an introduction.

H.J. I need more than that. I need grounds for *intimacy*.

MRS PREST. Well, then, say you want to be a lodger, a paying guest.

H.J. (*slowly*) It is not generally supposed easy for women to rise to the large, free view of a matter but they sometimes throw off a brilliant conception.

MRS PREST. We have our uses.

H.J. How shall we begin?

MRS PREST (*pointedly*) You will begin. By—writing them a short note. Do you think they will know your name?

H.J. No, but I will change that.

MRS PREST. What about your letters?

H.J. My publisher will bombard me with letters addressed to me in my feigned name. My banker will take in my real letters and I shall go every day to collect them. It will give me a little walk.

MRS PREST. Well, you and your publisher are a precious pair. I suppose it occurs to you that in spite of all your pains they may still suspect you of being his emissary?

(*There is a pause*)

H.J. (*moving down* L) Yes—and I see only one way to parry that.

MRS PREST. And what may that be?

H.J. I'm not sure I should tell you.

MRS PREST. I call that a little ungrateful.

H.J. (*turning to her*) I'm sorry for it, but there's no baseness I would not commit for the sake of Jeffrey Aspern's papers.

MRS PREST (*amused*) You won't murder the poor women, I hope?

H.J. (*shaking his head; with a smile*) I may not have the tradition of personal conquest, Helen, but any man—if he desires something enough, can put himself in the running, you said so yourself just now.

MRS PREST. The "if" is a big one.

H.J. The stake is big.

MRS PREST. Don't be such a tease, Henry Jarvis. What is your stake?

H.J. My stake is to make love to the niece.

(MRS PREST *turns towards the landing. As she approaches the steps it can be seen that her shoulders are shaking with suppressed laughter)*

(*He moves* c) What are you laughing at? Helen, please! (*He crosses to* l *of her*) Why are you laughing?

MRS PREST. Never mind! Wait till you've seen her. (*She goes on to the landing and her laughter mounts*) Wait till you've seen her!

(MRS PREST *exits down the stairs.* H.J. *stands for a moment looking after her. He looks towards the windows up* L, *hesitates, then goes on to the landing*)

H.J. (*calling quietly down the stairs*) If you will excuse me, Helen, I will wait five minutes longer. I have an idea.

(*There is no answer but the slam of the front door.*

H.J. *pauses for a second, shrugs his shoulders, crosses to the table* LC *and puts down his hat, stick and gloves. He goes to the french windows up* L *and opens the shutters. The sala fills with the cool, clear light of a late afternoon in April.* H.J. *looks out then exits to the balcony. His steps are heard going down the iron stairs into the garden. The bells from the nearby campanile ring out three-quarters of an hour and are echoed by other bells. The last to strike is cracked and jars the romantic noise. Almost immediately one of the double doors is opened. It creaks prodigiously.*

MISS TINA *enters up* C. *She is a long, lean, pale person. Her face is not young, but candid; not fresh, but clear. She has large eyes which are not bright, and a great deal of brownish, dull hair which is carelessly dressed. Her strong but sensitive hands are not noticeably clean. Her grey dress is fully ten years out of fashion. She wears a black scarf on her head in the Italian style. Her slippers are of raffia, and when she moves they oblige her to scuffle slightly. A chatelaine hangs on a chain at her waist and a silver cross at her neck. She looks towards the landing, listens for a few moments, then crosses and looks out of the landing window. She turns towards the double doors, notices that the shutters are open and turns to the stairs*)

TINA (*calling softly down the stairs*) Assunta! (*She crosses and stands up* C)

(ASSUNTA *enters up the stairs and comes into the room*)

Assunta why are the shutters . . .?

(TINA *breaks off as* ASSUNTA *puts her finger dramatically to her lips.* TINA, *puzzled, goes slightly towards her.* ASSUNTA, *clutching her throat, mimes that someone is "out there in the garden".* TINA *gives a frightened look towards the french windows, but from where she is standing she cannot see down into the garden*)

ASSUNTA. In giardino!

TINA (*whispering*) But I heard the door slam, I thought they had gone.

ASSUNTA (*whispering*) One gone. One stay. (*She points to H.J.'s hat and stick on the table*)

(TINA *has not seen a smart top-hat in this house for years, and she approaches it as if it were a large black spider which she has to kill. She picks it up gingerly and looks inside. H.J.'s gloves fall out of the hat which makes her start*)

(*She approaches the table, looking wonderingly at Miss Tina, takes the hat from her and looks inside*) Londra. Inglese!

(*At this moment* H.J.'s *footsteps are heard ascending from the garden.* ASSUNTA *and* TINA *stand in panic for a moment, then* TINA *moves towards the double doors up* C. ASSUNTA, *still holding the hat, goes towards the landing. As* TINA *reaches the doors she notices the hat and hisses at* ASSUNTA *who stops, turns and looks at her.* TINA, *with a quick glance to see that* H.J. *has not already reached the window, snatches the hat from Assunta, hissing again that she should go*)

(*She goes on to the landing, muttering*) Santo Dio!

(ASSUNTA *exits rapidly down the stairs.* TINA *quickly replaces the hat on the table* LC, *but the wrong way up. She turns towards the double doors and after a pace or two, she turns back to the table and corrects this mistake. She once more moves to the double doors.* H.J. *enters from the balcony*)

H.J. (*with intense excitement*) Per favore! Il giardino. Mi faccia il piacere di dirmi che'l giardino e il suo!

TINA (*standing up* C) No, no, the garden is not mine. Nothing here is mine.

H.J. (*moving to* L *of Tina and taking her hand; disingenuously*) Ah! But you're English! How delightful!

(H.J. *offers to shake her hand.* TINA *reluctantly permits this but when, as an afterthought,* H.J. *then wishes to kiss her hand, she withdraws it and hides it by wrapping it in her shawl*)

(*After a pause*) This is deplorable! What must you think of me?

(TINA *does not reply*)

(*He crosses below Tina to the landing and looks out of the window*) Hasn't my gondola come yet? (*He glances at his watch*) He promised he would be here—oh, an age ago. (*He turns to Tina*) What must you think of me? How *did* it all happen? (*He moves up* RC, *starts to improvise wildly but tries at the same time to sound cheerful and urbane*) Yes, that was it—*I* was going *down* the Grand Canal when I saw our mutual friend—Mrs Prest, and her friends coming *up* it—though I am never quite sure which is up and which is down the Grand Canal—are you? Ha, ha!

(TINA *does not respond to this lame joke*)

Well, we halted our gondolas and, since we had not seen each other for some time, I stepped into *hers* offering to accompany them wherever they might be going. *They* said they were coming *here*, and so on we came. (*He looks at Tina to see how she is taking this*)

(TINA'S *expression, though not incredulous, is extremely puzzled. This throws H.J. from his train of invention for a moment*)

(*He moves to* R *of Tina*) And this is what is so extraordinary—while we were on the way here I told the Contessa—Mrs Prest's friend—that I was looking for a modest palazzo to rent for the Summer. To my simple amazement she said she had a spare one herself, which she occasionally rents. "Ah, but my dear lady," I said to her, "has it a garden? Or at the very least, a large, flowering terrace?" (*He looks at Tina to see if she is following his, so far, plausible tergiversations and lies. He is determined to get a word out of her*)

TINA (*after a pause*) Has it?

H.J. No, it has not.

TINA (*pointing to the garden*) There are no flowers to speak of down there.

H.J. There are quite a few, reckless marguerites. (*He moves a little down* C) I am intending to be in Venice all Summer. Perhaps longer. I have some reading and study ahead of me, and that is why I felt I must be quiet. I don't need exercise, but I do need the open air. That's why I've felt a garden to be really indispensable. I'm sure you'll agree?

TINA (*moving to* L *of H.J.*) I've told you, the garden doesn't belong to me.

H.J. But it belongs to the house?

TINA. Oh, yes.

H.J. Well, then?

(TINA *clasps her hands convulsively in front of her, glances at them and seeing they are not clean, reclasps them behind her back*)

TINA. Oh, don't take it away from us. We like it. I like it.

H.J. Do you use it?

TINA. Not often. But I like to know it's there.

H.J. Of course you do. It's absurd, if you like, for a man—but I can't live without flowers.

TINA. Oh, we have a few flowers later on. (*She looks towards the garden, then at H.J.*) That trellis of roses needs pruning. It doesn't bloom for long, but when it does it is very pretty.

H.J. (*quoting*)

"I have a garden of my own,
But so with roses overblown,
And lilies, that you would it guess
To be a little wilderness."

TINA (*flatly*) We don't have any lilies. The soil here is old and used up. (*She pauses*) Like the house, I suppose. You've no idea how much it costs to buy new soil and bring it from *terra firma*, from the Veneto. And besides, you need a man.

H.J. (*gaily*) Why shouldn't I be the man?

(TINA *looks at him, frightened*)

I mean, I'd pay for the gardener. (*He crosses below her to the french windows*) You shall have the sweetest flowers in all Venice. And we will prune the vine and that old magnolia, and soon, soon the magnolia will be thrusting its pink and white petals into the air and the sun—(*he turns and moves up* R *of the table*) and people passing on the water will gaze at it, like the great Omar, and say:

> "But still a Ruby kindles in the Vine,
> And still a Garden by the Water blows."

TINA. I don't think we should like people gazing. (*She crosses above H.J. to the french windows and looks out*)

(*There is a pause*)

H.J. (*looking at his watch; nonplussed*) I wonder if my fool of a gondolier has found this place at last.

(*But H.J. does not go to look. Instead he holds her with his eyes. TINA's expression changes. She turns her back on him and gazes out at the garden*)

TINA. But we don't know you.

H.J. (*with a step towards her*) True, we don't even know each other's name. We start equal. But if you're English I can say I'm almost a fellow-countryman.

TINA (*turning sharply to face him*) We're not English.

H.J. (*as if amazed with admiration*) You speak the language so beautifully.

(TINA *looks blankly at him*)

You don't mean, by any chance, that you also are an American?

TINA. I don't know. We used to be.

H.J. How do you mean?

TINA. It's so many years ago. We don't seem to be anything now.

H.J. You mean you have lived here for so many years? (*He senses that this question is also too direct and turns away*) Well, I don't wonder at that. (*He moves* C) It's a grand old house. I suppose all the family like to use the garden?

TINA. The family?

H.J. As many as you are . . .

TINA (*moving to* L *of H.J.*) There's only one other than me.

H.J. (*turning to her*) Only two of you—in all this great house.

But, dear lady, there must be at least thirty rooms. Surely, surely you could let me two or three of them.

Tina. What for?

H.J. (*after a second's pause*) For a good rent.

(*There is a pause*)

Tina. I mean—"why"?

H.J. Because—I have business to do in Venice (*He moves* RC) Work in Venice. Friends in Venice. And I need a garden—also in Venice. Like most expatriate Americans, I am a migrant bird. (*He turns and takes a step towards her*) At each change of the seasons I look for a new, faraway nest.

Tina. What do you do?

H.J. Do?

Tina. Do—when you are not looking for nests.

H.J. (*temporizing with a chuckle*) Ah, what a shrewd sense of humour you have. Well—someday, perhaps you will permit me to tell you of all that. It is work of a—well—chiefly of a personal nature. I need time for study, I need quiet, stillness, and for health's sake, some fresh air.

Tina. You cannot find these things where you come from?

H.J. In America? Yes, I suppose there is still fresh air in America. Quiet and stillness in the mountains of Vermont or the Arizona desert. But for my work further conditions are required. I need an aura of history and the sense of the past. America is a great country, but she is still so bewitchingly—so heartrendingly —young. America is agog for history. The rustle of the corn, the whisper of the long grass, the very buds as they burst open in the Spring, deafen your ears with the sound of America's history still unborn. I cannot wait for that. By soul I am a European. I may pay my respects to posterity. I cannot ignore the here and now, but for me the present and the future are both rooted in the past— (*he turns up stage and moves towards the landing*) and here, where the long arm of the Adriatic sweeps up to embrace the city which is his bride, I find all my conditions fulfilled—if only I may have a garden. (*He turns to face Tina*) Do you see what I mean?

Tina (*simply*) You mean, Venice is old.

H.J. (*moving to* R *of her*) I mean, do you think you could rent me the rooms?

Tina (*turning away* L) I should have to ask my aunt.

H.J. (*smiling, as if he had not heard*) I beg your pardon?

Tina (*turning to him*) Miss Bordereau. I shall have to ask her.

H.J. Will she be back soon?

Tina. Oh, no. She is asleep in there. I was reading to her when you all arrived and shortly afterwards she fell asleep.

H.J. (*somewhat too sternly*) The maid said you were at church.

Tina (*embarrassed*) I did not tell her to say that.

H.J. Your aunt—she is not ill, I hope?

TINA. She rests all the time. That's why I never leave the house.

H.J. I shall look forward to her acquaintance. When do you think you could ask her?

TINA (*moving above the table* LC) We're very poor, we live very badly—almost on nothing. (*She indicates the room*) Look! You see, we've sold almost everything there is to sell.

(H.J. *is silent, feeling that victory is within grasp*)

But flowers! Oh, my goodness, *flowers!* (*She moves about as if released from a spell, and stands down* L. *of the table*) If we could make the garden and the house look even just a little like it looked in the old days. Flowers in the house again. Oh, what bliss!

H.J. (*moving to* R *of the table* LC) It will be my privilege to provide them for you. To watch your face as it is now will, occasionally, be my reward. You have told me your aunt's name. What is yours?

TINA (*the smile draining from her face*) Everyone calls me "Miss Tina".

H.J. Miss Tina?

(TINA *nods*)

That is a very charming name.

(TINA's *smile lights up again, but when she finds* H.J. *gazing at her, it drains away*)

What do you say, Miss Tina?

TINA. But we've never done anything of the sort. We've never taken in lodgers, I mean . . .

(H.J. *starts to speak*)

(*She over-rides him*) No, please listen. Most of the rooms are very bare. There's nothing at all in some of them. I don't know how you'd sleep. How you'd live. (*She is near tears, but laughs like a schoolgirl*) Isn't it dreadful?

(H.J. *is now certain that his conquest has begun. For the rest of the scene he switches on the quiet charm of a friend who is used to dealing with family troubles*)

H.J. (*chuckling*) It's not dreadful at all. (*He crosses to* RC) With your permission—and that of your aunt—I could easily put in a few tables and chairs. C'est la moindre des choses. My manservant and my gondolier can bring the things round as soon as you give me the word.

TINA. I don't know what my aunt will say.

H.J. (*moving to* R *of the table*) She will probably consider the whole thing very *louche*. But I shall depend on you.

TINA. I shouldn't do that.

H.J. Well, then, on the flowers.

TINA. Oh, no! On the money!

(*For a moment this causes H.J. to lose his sense of "personal conquest" and his look of friendliness narrows sharply. His eyes have not left her face*)

H.J. (*picking up his hat, stick and gloves*) When will you talk to your aunt?

TINA (*turning away up* LC) Tonight.

H.J. And when will you let me know?

TINA. Tomorrow. If I can.

H.J. (*crossing to* L *of Tina*) Tomorrow? At what time?

TINA. About three o'clock.

H.J. I should call here at three o'clock?

TINA (*moving* C) I may keep you waiting a little.

H.J. If I may feel that *you* favour the idea the wait will be endurable. (*He looks at his watch then takes a step towards her*) I must go now. (*He puts his hand out as if to shake hers*) Au revoir! A demain!

(TINA *makes no move*)

(*He crosses above Tina to the landing*) Please do not trouble yourself to see me out.

TINA (*suddenly; for she has been saving this up*) You haven't told me your name. (*She moves to* L *of him*)

H.J. Oh, how stupid of me.

(H.J.'s *hand automatically reaches for his visiting card. He brings it out and is about to present it when he recollects himself*)

Oh, no, that's somebody else's. Henry Jessamine, Miss Tina. Mr Henry Jessamine.

TINA. Jessamine? *That's* a flower, isn't it?

H.J. (*eagerly*) That reminds me: what are your favourite, your truly favourite flowers?

TINA (*without hesitation*) Roses, of course.

H.J. What colour?

TINA (*gaily*) What does the colour matter?

H.J. Red?

(TINA *nods her head ecstatically. A spring bell at the head of the stairs rings shrilly*)

TINA (*panic stricken*) It's my aunt's bell. Forgive me.

(TINA *turns to exit by the double doors, but leaves one slipper behind. She and H.J. both go to pick it up but H.J. gets there first. He hands it to* TINA *and she hurries out in confusion up* C, *closing the doors. H.J., left alone, tiptoes swiftly to the double doors. At this moment* ASSUNTA *is heard coming up the stairs. H.J. moves quickly up* L.

ASSUNTA *enters on the landing*)

ASSUNTA (*gruffly*) The signore is going?

H.J. I rather think Miss Tina expects me to stay-- (*he crosses down* R) but I must be off soon. (*He looks at his watch to give this lie a faint colour*)

(ASSUNTA *goes to the double doors and opens one. It creaks as usual*)

TINA (*off*) Yes?

ASSUNTA. Assunta.

TINA (*off; calling*) It's all right. I'll be out in a minute. Has the American gentleman gone?

ASSUNTA. No.

TINA. Ask him to wait, please.

ASSUNTA (*closing the door and moving down* C) You will wait here, please. Make yourself at home.

H.J. The old lady--she is not ill, I hope?

ASSUNTA. She will see us all buried. (*She moves towards the landing*)

(TINA *enters up* C, *smiling*)

TINA. Assunta, go in and look after my aunt.

(ASSUNTA *exits up* C, *leaving the door open*)

(*She moves down* C) Isn't it fortunate? She woke up. One can hear nothing from her bedroom at the back, but she said she sensed there were visitors.

H.J. I hope she isn't displeased that I have over-stayed your most charming welcome. (*He puts his hat, stick and gloves on the chair down* R)

TINA. Oh, I don't think so at all. I told her of your plan.

H.J. (*turning sharply to her*) My plan?

TINA. About the rooms.

H.J. Oh! What did she say?

TINA (*eagerly*) She said she'd like to see you. It's so unlike her. Well, no, it isn't really. She hates appointments and she gave up her tea parties long ago but sometimes, if someone calls, she suddenly wants to meet them. Isn't it strange?

H.J. Not at all. Very understandable.

(MISS JULIANA BORDEREAU *in her wheel chair, is pushed on up* C *by* ASSUNTA. JULIANA *is a very small, shrunken figure, bent forward a little, with her hands in her lap. She is dressed in a black gown and shawl which look almost beetle-green with the patina of age. She wears a dark green eye shade, and over her head is an old black lace mantilla. Only her chin, mouth and nose are visible; the eyes and every trace of hair are hidden. Despite this, the tiny, still figure is impressive. She speaks in a thin, weak voice which has an agreeable, cultured sound.* TINA *goes to the wheel chair and takes over from Assunta.*)

ASSUNTA *closes the double doors, then exits down the stairs* R.
TINA *wheels Juliana down* C, *and looks round as if to see if there
might be a draught somewhere. She also manages to give H.J. a small
smile. During the ensuing conversation* TINA *remains standing behind
the wheel chair*)

(*After a pause*) I hope I see you well, Miss Bordereau.
JULIANA. As well as you will ever see me, sir.
H.J. This is kind of you.
JULIANA. How so?
H.J. (*raising his voice and approaching her*) Kind of you to leave
your sanctum to meet a stranger.
JULIANA. I can hear quite well. Please to sit down.

(H.J. *glances at* TINA *who gives him a nervous smile. He then sits
on the chair up* R, *pulling it slightly to* C)

H.J. Thank you.
JULIANA. Sanctum? Is it my parlour you mean, or my bedroom?

(H.J. *looks nonplussed and glances again at* TINA. *She smiles and
while still looking at him conspiratorially bends over Juliana as a nurse
might with her patient*)

TINA. I don't think we're quite awake yet, are we?
JULIANA (*with sudden sharpness*) We are wide-awake and we
don't need you cawing like a crow over our shoulder. Tina, go in
and write that letter to the lawyer. You know what I mean.
TINA (*moving to the doors up* C) Yes, Auntie.

(H.J. *rises and moves to the doors up* C)

JULIANA. Write it neatly.
TINA (*quite deflated*) Yes, Auntie.

(TINA *exits up* C. H.J. *resumes his seat*)

JULIANA. Our house is not fashionable. It is far from the centre.
But this canal is still very *comme il faut*.
H.J. It is the sweetest corner of Venice. I can imagine nothing
more charming.

(JULIANA *utters a small noise and seems to toss her head slightly*)

JULIANA. Miss Tina tells me you want to buy the house.
H.J. No, no! I did not suggest that.
JULIANA. What then?
H.J. How shall I begin?
JULIANA. At the beginning.
H.J. Well, first and foremost, there is the garden.
JULIANA. Go on.
H.J. It was a case of love at first sight.
JULIANA (*expressionlessly*) Indeed.

H.J. You have been here so long—you cannot realize the impression it makes on a stranger. I felt it was a case to risk something. I hope that your kindness in receiving me is a sign that I am not wholly out in my calculation.

JULIANA. I cannot imagine what you are talking about, Mr —er . . .?

H.J. Jessamine. Henry Jessamine.

JULIANA. You are American? You don't sound like an American.

H.J. If you will permit me to say so, neither do you. Nor does that lady—is she your niece?

JULIANA (*disregarding the question*) If you're so fond of a garden why don't you lodge on the mainland? There are many gardens on *terra firma* far better than this.

H.J. But don't you understand? It's the idea of a garden in the middle of the sea.

JULIANA. This isn't the middle of the sea. You can't even see the water. (*She slowly removes her eye shade*)

(*There is a long pause. H.J. gazes at Juliana*)

H.J. But, my dear lady, I came up to your very gate in my boat.

JULIANA. Yes, if you've got a boat. (*She sounds vague and distant and as if she had suddenly lost her energy*) It's many years since I have been in one of the gondole.

H.J. (*eagerly*) Let me assure you that my pleasure would be to put mine at your service.

JULIANA. Miss Tina tells me you talked with her a long time.

H.J. Miss Tina has been very patient with me.

JULIANA. She has very good manners. I brought her up myself.

H.J. Ah! . . . (*He tails off, unable to enlarge the compliment*)

JULIANA (*suddenly*) I don't know who you may be, sir——

H.J. I was just about to tell you . . .

JULIANA (*overlapping*) —and I don't want to know. It signifies very little. Very little today. Miss Tina tells me you are a good talker. Folk now-a-days don't know what "talk" means. You may have as many rooms as you like if you will pay me a good deal of money.

(H.J. *is dumb for a moment*)

H.J. I will pay with pleasure and of course in advance whatever you think it proper to ask of me.

JULIANA (*without hesitation*) Well then, a thousand lire a month.

(H.J. *looks startled for a moment but composes himself*)

What do you say to that?

H.J. I say your views on the matter perfectly meet with my own.

(JULIANA *gives a soft grunt*)

(*He springs to his feet*) Then that is settled.

JULIANA. Not quite settled. When will you pay me?

H.J. Let me see—tomorrow—may I, tomorrow, have the pleasure of placing a month's rent in your hand?

JULIANA. You may.

H.J. (*feeling that she is being altogether too grasping*) Of course it is a slight matter, but I have not yet seen the rooms you propose for me.

JULIANA. Tomorrow, when you bring the money.

H.J. But supposing . . .

JULIANA. You will like the rooms well enough. More important people than you have liked them.

H.J. I only meant that a glimpse of them might give me some notion of what I should need to . . .

JULIANA. Sir! If you are going to haggle, the matter is closed.

(TINA *opens the door up* c *a fraction, hardly shows herself and whispers apologetically*)

TINA. I am sorry to interrupt. Is the letter to be to Signor Pochintesta or to his partner?

JULIANA. Come in.

(TINA *comes into the room and closes the door behind her*)

H.J. (*moving towards Tina*) It is all settled.

JULIANA. He seems to think I am trying to sell him a pig in a poke.

(TINA *moves to* L *of the wheel chair*)

He is haggling.

H.J. (*moving and standing behind his chair*) On the contrary . . .

JULIANA. You'd think he'd come here to do *us* a favour.

H.J. My dear Miss Bordereau! (*He swallows his pride*) I am exceedingly sorry that I should have given you such an impression. Everything shall be entirely as you wish.

JULIANA (*almost gaily*) He'll give three thousand. Three thousand tomorrow.

H.J. I see. Three months in advance.

JULIANA. That was what you said, wasn't it?

H.J. (*patiently*) Of course.

TINA (*looking from one to the other*) Do you mean *lire*?

JULIANA. Dollars or *lire*?

H.J. (*smiling sturdily*) I think lire is what we said.

TINA. That's very good, all the same.

JULIANA (*with a soft coldness*) What do you know? You're ignorant.

TINA. Oh, yes. Of money I am—certainly of money.

H.J. I'm sure you have your own fine branches of knowledge. (*With a reckless gaiety*) Dollars, lire, roubles or pounds—who cares?

JULIANA. She had a good education when she was young. I saw to that myself. But she has learned nothing since.
TINA (*mildly*) I have always been with *you*.
JULIANA. Yes, *but for that* . . .

(TINA *blushes*)

(*To H.J.*) And what time did you say you'd bring the money?
H.J. Whenever you say. I shall have to visit the bank. If it suits you, I'll come at noon.
JULIANA. I'm always here, but I have my hours.
H.J. You mean the times you receive?
JULIANA. I never receive. But I'll see you at noon.
H.J. Very good.
JULIANA. With the money.
H.J. I think we have made *that* point quite clear. (*He moves to* R *of the wheel chair*) May we shake hands on our contract?

(JULIANA *makes no movement*)

(*He repeats his request in a perceptible tone of emotion*) Miss Bordereau, may I, to seal this moment, shake your hand? (*He offers his hand*)
JULIANA (*ignoring H.J.'s hand*) I belong to a time when that was not the custom.

(H.J. *is at a loss for a moment but turns to Tina*)

H.J. Oh, you'll do as well. (*He forcefully wrings Tina's hand*)
TINA (*fluttering*) Yes, yes. Just to show we're all friends.

(JULIANA *makes her first gesture*)

JULIANA. Tina!
TINA. Yes, Auntie? (*She releases H.J.'s hand and starts to wheel Juliana out. She pushes the chair down stage and backwards down* L *to face H.J.*)

(H.J. *bows.*
ASSUNTA *enters up the stairs, crosses to the double doors and opens them.* JULIANA *raises her hand.* TINA *stops the wheel chair*)

JULIANA. Shall you bring the money in gold?
H.J. Aren't you a little afraid, after all, of keeping such a sum as that in the house?
JULIANA. Of whom should I be afraid, if not of you?
H.J. (*laughing easily*) In point of fact I shall be a protector. I'll bring you gold if you prefer.
JULIANA. Yes. Do. (*She gives a curt nod of the head, indicating dismissal*)

(H.J. *bows.* TINA *pushes the wheel chair up* C.
ASSUNTA, *at a gesture from* TINA, *wheels Juliana off up* C. TINA *closes the double doors*)

H.J. (*moving to Tina*) I've had better fortune than I dared to hope.

(TINA *and* H.J. *move down* C, H.J. *is* R *of Tina*)

TINA. Is it so important to you? It's such a little matter.

H.J. It's a little garden but no little matter.

TINA. You seem so excited.

H.J. Do I? I hope I did not alarm your aunt?

TINA. She is not easily alarmed.

H.J. Did you put in a good word for me?

TINA (*shaking her head*) I had no time. No, it was the idea of the money. I told her I thought you were rich.

H.J. And what put that into your head?

TINA. The way you talked.

H.J. Dear me, I must talk differently now. I'm sorry to say it's not the case.

TINA. Well, I think that in Venice foreigners often give a great deal for something that after all isn't much.

H.J. A truer word was never spoken.

(H.J. *picks up his gloves and cane and once more paces round the room*)

Ah, but this is a fine room. Certainly a fine room in its way.

TINA. I do not like it and in winter it is cold.

H.J. (*cheerfully*) A room cannot have all the virtues. (*He moves to the french windows*) It's coolness is a benison now.

TINA. Will you let me know something?

H.J. (*turning to face her*) If it is within my knowledge.

TINA. Do all writers talk the way you do?

H.J. Writers?

TINA. Yes. Authors. *You* know.

H.J. (*moving to* R *of the table* LC) Oh, you mean my bookwork. Ah, yes, well—I am a very minor, very humble scribbler. A bit of an historian, a bit of an essayist. I imagine my enemies call me a dilettante and my friends an amateur. When they come to write my obituary I suppose I shall go down as a man of letters.

TINA. You mean they'll write a piece about you when you die? In the papers? Then you must be famous.

H.J. (*moving to* L *of her*) Ah, no! Fame, true fame, is for the very few. There will be a paragraph or two. Perhaps—three paragraphs. I only hope they are written by the right man. (*He senses he has got on to dangerous ground*) But let us not talk about me. What were we saying? Oh, yes, this room. (*He turns to the windows and back*) Will it, do you suppose, form part of my *quartiere*?

(H.J.'*s boldness dumbfounds* TINA)

TINA. Not if you go above—to the second floor.

H.J. I infer that is where your aunt would like me to be.

TINA. She said your apartment ought to be very distinct. But whenever you use the garden or are on your way upstairs—(*she gestures to the garden with one hand and the stairs with the other*) you will be free to use this room.

(H.J. *does not answer but looks vaguely upward*)

(*She moves to* R *of him*) Please do not ask me to show the other rooms now. They are all unswept and I'm afraid there's a large bird's nest in one of them, but we'll soon get all that seen to. They used to be very fine rooms.

(*There is a slight pause.* H.J. *again does not answer. He is wondering whether the game is worth the candle. He makes a small, deprecatory gesture*)

I don't know whether it will make any difference to you, but the money is for me.

H.J. The money?

TINA. The money you are going to bring.

H.J. You'll make me want to stay here two or three years.

TINA. That would be good for me.

H.J. You put me on my honour.

TINA. She wants me to have more. She thinks she's going to die.

H.J. Not soon, I hope!

TINA. One can never tell. She says she's tired of living and she would like to die—"for a change". All her friends are dead. She says she ought to have gone too, or else one or two of the nice ones should have stayed. But she thinks that when I'm alone I shall be a great fool and not know how to manage. (*Suddenly*) People don't just die when they want to, do they?

H.J. (*crossing above Tina and picking up his hat*) It is certainly not the general rule. She—er—seemed—how shall I say—a little suspicious of me.

TINA (*turning to him*) How can you say that, when she let you in so easily?

H.J. You call that "easily"? What possible advantage could I take of either of you? (*He moves towards the landing*)

TINA. I oughtn't to tell you even if I knew, ought I? (*She turns outwards to up* C, *to face* H.J.) Do you . . . I mean do you think we have any weak points?

H.J. If you had you would only have to mention them for me to respect them religiously.

TINA. But there's nothing to tell. We're terribly quiet. I don't know how the days pass. We have no life.

H.J. (*with a step towards her*) I should like to think I might bring you a little.

TINA. Oh, we know what we want. It's all right.

H.J. (*moving closer to her*) Well, don't you be too proud—or shy. Don't hide away from me altogether.

Tina. Oh, I have to stay with my aunt. I must.

H.J. And I must go now. (*He holds out his hand*)

Tina (*impulsively*) Don't you think it's too much?

(H.J. *looks questioningly at her*)

Don't you think the money is too much?

H.J. (*taking her hand and holding it firmly*) That will depend. Oh yes, that will depend—on the *pleasure* I get out of it.

(Tina *looks away*)

Tina. Oh, pleasure, pleasure—there's no pleasure in this house.

H.J. *kisses her hand.* Tina *turns to him in astonishment. He releases her hand, bows again and goes to the landing. He starts to go down the stairs.* Tina *remains gazing after him, her hand still in mid-air, motionless, as—*

the Curtain *falls*

ACT II

SCENE I

SCENE—*The same. Six weeks later. Afternoon.*

When the CURTAIN *rises there has been some change in the furniture. The circular table is now* RC *and has upright chairs* R, L *and above it, and it is covered with a red chenille cloth. An upholstered "sociable" couch is* LC. *The console table up* LC *is now the right way up. A small pedestal table stands down* R *and there is a tall pedestal above the french windows and a small chair below them. The whole room is a little more like itself and looks warmer than it has before. Perhaps it is the summer sun which streams in through the french windows, but what most strikes the eye is a profusion of flowers; they are everywhere, in great summer bunches, a vase of roses on the table down* R, *a vase of roses on the table* RC, *a vase of roses on the pedestal up* L *and vases of mixed flowers on the console tables* R *and* L *of the double doors.* ASSUNTA *is by the table* RC, *squinting inquisitively at the letters and parcels of newspapers which lie there unopened. Her rag bandage at her throat is gone.* PASQUALE *enters down the stairs* R *and stops on the landing, watching Assunta examining the envelopes. Rope-soled shoes help him to do this silently.* PASQUALE *is* H.J.'*s temporary manservant, and is a spry, neat fellow of indeterminate age. He speaks excellent English, is observant and intelligent. He is, however, a social snob. He is most respectful to his temporary master but the arrangements, or lack of them, in this household distress him. He is anxious to leave Italy and be in service again in England, as he once was. America, he thinks, might suit him even better. He is so fiercely Anglophile that he insists on speaking English even to Assunta. He is carrying* H.J.'*s tail suit which he will press in the kitchen.*

PASQUALE (*after a pause; quietly*) Are you expecting a love letter, Assunta? (*He moves and stands above the table* RC)
ASSUNTA (*looking up and dropping the letters negligently on the table*) Io? No! (*She crosses to* C)

(PASQUALE *puts the suit on the chair above the table and arranges the letters and packets in the way he likes to see them*)

Dov'e il padrone?
PASQUALE. My master is out.
ASSUNTA. E quando torna?
PASQUALE (*taking a nail file from his pocket*) Mr Jessamine did not say when he would be back. (*He files his nails*) He has been out all day. Why do you not polish your English, Assunta, like I do?

26

Then perhaps one day you can go to England, like I have done with Lord Buckstone. Or even America.

(ASSUNTA *looks placidly at Pasquale. She thinks him a little cracked.* PASQUALE *finishes rearranging the letters, picks up the suit and as he turns to go he glances at* ASSUNTA *standing in the middle of the sala, mopping her forehead with her apron*)

What are you waiting about here for?

ASSUNTA. Sono in giardino.

PASQUALE (*crossing above Assunta to the french windows; excitedly*) So they are in the garden at last!

ASSUNTA. Vogliono sapere quando lui torni. Vogliono evitarlo.

PASQUALE (*turning to her*) Why do they want to avoid Mr Jessamine? (*He turns back and looks out of the windows*)

ASSUNTA (*mimicking his English*) Why you do not ask them? (*She moves to* R *of him*) C'e troppo spionaggio in questa casa.

PASQUALE (*turning to her*) Spionaggio! I am no spy. The padrone has taken much trouble with the garden. (*He crosses to the landing*) Each day he asks me—"Have the ladies seen the garden yet?"

ASSUNTA. They can see it from their windows.

PASQUALE. It is not polite. It makes him very hurt. (*He turns, to go upstairs. At the landing window he looks out*) He is coming now.

(ASSUNTA *moves towards the french windows*)

(*He calls sharply*) Assunta!

(ASSUNTA *stops*)

Don't tell them. Let him make politeness with them. Let him say "Buon giorno" at least. (*He operates the front door mechanism*)

ASSUNTA. No! No! *You* don't tell *him*. Let him go upstairs. Then you help us wheel her in. Pasquale!

PASQUALE. Don't go. Don't tell them!

(ASSUNTA *gives him a piteous look but stays where she is.* PASQUALE *exits swiftly down the stairs* R *and we hear him open the door and the start of hurried conversation with H.J. below.* ASSUNTA'S *anxiety mounts as she hears this. Her fear of Juliana is greater than her regard for niceties of behaviour. She goes out on to the balcony and exits to the garden*)

(*Off*) The ladies are in the garden, sir.

(H.J.'s *steps are heard running up the stairs and he appears on the landing, a little breathless and very hot. He is dressed in a light, shantung suit and carries a panama hat, gloves and stick*)

H.J. (*calling*) Thank you, Pasquale, I will ring for you when I need you. (*He puts his stick and gloves and hat on the table up* RC)

PASQUALE (*off*) Very good, sir.

(H.J. *crosses to the french windows, peers out for a few seconds, then straightens up, mops his brow and goes to the doors up* C. *He looks at the doors, and for a moment he is riveted. Evidently there is no immediate danger, for he tries the doors and attempts to open one of them. It does not yield*)

H.J. (*under his breath*) Devils! (*He stoops and tries to look through the keyhole of the doors up* C.)

(PASQUALE *enters silently up the stairs* R, *still carrying the suit. He is just in time to see H.J. at the keyhole. He watches in quiet amazement.*
      H.J. *crouches to get a better view*)

PASQUALE (*very quietly*) I said the ladies are in the garden, sir.

(H.J. *rises and wheels round. He is completely flummoxed for a moment*)

H.J. Oh, did you? I thought you said Miss Bordereau was in the garden. I thought I should possibly find Miss Tina in the parlour.

PASQUALE. No, milord. They are all of them down in the garden.

H.J. (*moving and sitting* L *of the table* RC) Ah, well. I won't disturb them. Perhaps I will wait here so that I may pay my respects when they come in. (*He opens one of his letters*)

(PASQUALE *just stands there*)

That's all, Pasquale. I will ring for you when I need you.

PASQUALE (*moving above the table*) I only came to ask, milord, if you would need your tails this evening?

H.J. What? Yes—I don't know—probably. Press 'em, anyway. I may not go out this evening, until later. I may take a little nap this afternoon.

PASQUALE (*moving to* L *of H.J.*) At what time shall I call your Lordship?

(H.J. *looks at Pasquale*)

H.J. (*after a pause*) Pasquale, unless my ears deceive me that is the third time you have addressed me by a title which I could not possibly possess. I am a simple American. We have no "lords" where I come from. (*He reads a letter*)

PASQUALE (*carefully*) I only thought, Mr Jessamine, sir, that I would let you know that I, Pasquale, will respect your desire to travel incognito.

H.J. (*looking up sharply*) What on earth makes you think I am "travelling incognito"?

PASQUALE (*showing the tailor's label in the inside breast pocket of the evening suit*) "Henry Jarvis Esquire", sir, is the well-known

incognito of a much respected English nobleman. (*He bows*) Do
not be afraid. I quite understand why you wish to change it, Mr
Jessamine, sir.

H.J. (*at a loss*) Oh, you do, do you?

PASQUALE. Yes, sir, things have been--getting—a little bit
warm.

H.J. (*mopping his brow*) Not nearly as warm as they are now.

PASQUALE. Quite so, *sir*. I only thought you would like to know
that Pasquale you can trust.

H.J. I never doubted that for a moment. Thank you, Pasquale.

PASQUALE. Don't mench!

H.J. Will you go and see what they're up to now.

(PASQUALE *moves to the couch* LC, *puts down the suit, then goes
to the french windows and looks out*)

PASQUALE. Si, signore. They are folding the umbrella. I think
they are coming in. Shall I go to help them wheel the old lady
up the steps?

H.J. (*rising*) No. Let them sweat for a bit. (*He moves up* C) I
suppose they're only out there to calculate what my "improvements" are worth. Why have they never been out there before?
This is only the second time, in six weeks, that I have seen them.

PASQUALE. They like to keep quiet, sir.

H.J. It is more than keeping quiet. It is like hunted animals
feigning death. Heaven knows what mystic rites of ennui they
celebrate in those darkened rooms.

PASQUALE. They are here now, sir.

H.J. Thank you, Pasquale. (*He crosses to the french windows*)
Help them in.

(PASQUALE *goes on to the balcony and disappears*)

TINA (*off*) Gently, gently. Thank you, Pasquale. *Gently*.

H.J. (*at the window*) May I help?

TINA (*off*) No, thank you, we can manage.

(TINA, PASQUALE, ASSUNTA and JULIANA *in her wheel chair
appear on the balcony*. ASSUNTA *carries the large sun umbrella*)

H.J. Steady, Pasquale. Here, let me help.

(TINA *comes into the room which forces* H.J. *to stay inside*)

TINA (*almost sharply*) No, please, that is not necessary. But you
may open the parlour doors for us, if you would be so kind.

H.J. The parlour doors? Oh, yes. The parlour doors. (*He goes
to the double doors and makes a pretence of trying to open them*)

(ASSUNTA *and* PASQUALE *wheel* JULIANA *into the room*)

I think you have forgotten.

(TINA *moves up* L)

You must have locked them. (*He steps to her*) The parlour doors are locked. Have you the key?
TINA. No, they are not locked.

(ASSUNTA *crosses above Tina to the double doors*)

They stick. Pull the right one towards you and push on the left.

(PASQUALE *wheels Juliana down* L *of the couch and stops the chair, facing* R. ASSUNTA *opens the double doors*)

They have been that way for years.
H.J. (*muttering*) How stupid of me. I thought they were locked.
TINA. Assunta, run along and make some tea.
JULIANA. I do not wish for tea now.
TINA. I would like some, if you don't mind. Go along, Assunta.

(ASSUNTA *crosses and exits down the stairs* R)

JULIANA (*to Tina*) Why on earth should anyone think that to take the air in the garden I would lock my doors?
H.J. (*crossing to* R *of the couch*) I didn't think. I mean I just thought they were locked.
JULIANA. "Think", "thought", "didn't think" . . .!

(TINA *crosses to the wheel chair and takes it from Pasquale*)

TINA (*sharply*) Let us not talk now. You're tired. Thank you, Pasquale.

(PASQUALE *moves and stands* L *of the double doors*)

H.J. (*moving to* R *of the wheel chair and addressing Tina across it*) Miss Tina, when you have a moment I would appreciate a word or two with you.
TINA. I will be with you presently.

(TINA *wheels the chair towards the double doors.* PASQUALE *assists, holding the door.* H.J. *moves aside, then follows and stands up* R)

JULIANA. When you have your chat with the gentleman you must ask him why he thinks I should lock my doors.
TINA (*embarrassed*) Please, Auntie. It was just that he didn't think.

(TINA *pushes Juliana out up* C)

JULIANA (*as she goes*) Didn't think? I dare say. I dare say.

(PASQUALE *closes the doors, moves to the couch, picks up the suit and looks enquiringly at H.J.*)

H.J. I shan't be going out this evening, Pasquale. You may go, if you wish.
PASQUALE. Thank you, signore. (*He crosses towards the landing*)
H.J. (*moving above the table* RC) Oh, just one other thing. Fetch

me a glass of water, please. *Half* a glass. A medicine glass, if you can find one.

(PASQUALE *exits quickly down the stairs* R. H.J. *goes to the table* RC *and looks for something.. He remembers that it is in his pocket. He brings it out. It is a small chemist's phial, wrapped in paper and sealed. He opens it and puts it upright on the table, then crosses above the couch to* L *of it.*

PASQUALE *enters up the stairs* R *carrying a tray with a glass jug of water and a glass which he puts on the table* RC)

You will find a bottle of medicine on the table somewhere. Open it and pour some in the water.

(PASQUALE *picks up the phial. As he does so* H.J. *sits on the right end of the couch, staggering a little*)

PASQUALE. Is anything the matter, sir?
H.J. How many drops does it say? Three, I think. Look on the label.
PASQUALE (*reading the label*) "Tre."
H.J. Three, then. Pour them for me. My hand is a little shaky.

(PASQUALE *puts a little water in the glass and adds three drops from the phial of what might be sal volatile, for it clouds the water. He picks up the glass, crosses and hands it to* H.J.
TINA *enters up* C *in time to see* H.J. *sip his medicine*)

(*He shudders violently*) Beastly stuff, but I suppose I must finish it.
TINA (*moving down* C) What is the matter?

(H.J. *affects not to hear, breathes heavily and loosens his tie*)

(*She moves closer to H.J.*) Whatever is the matter?
H.J. I *am* so sorry about this. Pasquale, bring me a chair for my feet.

(PASQUALE *crosses to the chair* L, *picks it up, moves it below the couch and places it in position for H.J.*)

TINA. What is wrong?

(PASQUALE *puts* H.J.'s *feet up on the chair. Since it is an upright chair* H.J. *looks very uncomfortable and not a little ridiculous*)

H.J. Thank you, my good fellow. You may go now.

(PASQUALE *takes the glass from* H.J.)

PASQUALE. Don't mench! (*He crosses above Tina towards the landing*)
TINA (*looking wide-eyed at Pasquale*) Is he ill?
PASQUALE. His head went like this. Suddenly he was faint, so I gave him three drops of his medicine.

TINA. Does this often happen?

(PASQUALE *looks at* H.J. *who shakes his head*)

PASQUALE. First time, miss.

TINA. You may go now. I will stay.

(PASQUALE *exits down the stairs* R)

(*She moves to* R *of H.J.*) I expect it's the heat. You have been out all day.

H.J. I was at the doctor's this afternoon. My heart, it appears, is not as strong as it used to be. (*He gestures vaguely towards the stairs*) All those awful stairs . . .

TINA (*very distressed*) I didn't know you had a bad heart.

H.J. How should you? Since the first day I came here six weeks ago I have only seen you once, do you remember? On that second day you took that not inconsiderable sum of gold as if it were a penny loaf and disappeared, leaving Assunta to show me round my rooms.

TINA. My aunt was in a good mood at that moment. I was afraid she might change her mind.

H.J. But you persuaded her not to?

(TINA *looks embarrassed*)

Or was it the money?

TINA (*nodding*) I'm afraid it was. Do you think perhaps you should go upstairs and lie down?

H.J. (*removing his feet from the chair*) No, I feel better now.

TINA. Don't move. You must rest.

H.J. No, please sit down.

(TINA *sits reluctantly on the chair near H.J.*)

One flight of stairs I can assay. Not, I think, three. I fear I shall have to seek other quarters.

TINA. You want to go away?

H.J. I see no alternative. Do you?

(TINA *looks towards the double doors then back at H.J.*)

TINA. I shall have to ask my aunt. She is not in a good mood just now. She keeps asking me to go out, not to stay with her. She says I am a worry, a bore.

H.J. That is surely her pride. The more she needs you, the more she resents the need.

TINA. I don't understand it. Sometimes she will sit for hours together, not moving. Sometimes she is so still I fear she is dead. Then one day I left her for a minute or two and when I came back she was the other side of the room, looking for something.

H.J. (*sharply*) Looking for what?

TINA. I don't know. I don't know how she managed it. When we dress her she gives us no help at all.

(H.J. *sits up, apparently quite recovered*)

H.J. How did you persuade her into the garden?
TINA. I didn't. She persuaded me.
H.J. What did she think of my "improvements"?
TINA. I don't know. She just dozed off.
H.J. What did you think?
TINA (*smiling*) It was never nice till now.
H.J. If you think it so nice ... Forgive me, but I have sent you quantities of flowers all these weeks. No, they were not from the garden. That takes time. But I promised you the sweetest flowers in all Venice, and you have had them. I have become a little discouraged. It may be that I pay too much heed to common form —but I confess a word of recognition, even if only relayed by a servant, would have touched me in the right place.
TINA. But I didn't know they were for me.
H.J. They were for both of you. But the roses were more particularly for you.

(H.J. *has regained the same footing that he had when he first flirted with her.* TINA *is delighted but frightened*)

TINA (*abruptly*) Why in the world do you want so much to know us?
H.J. That is your aunt's question, not yours.
TINA (*shaking her head*) She didn't tell me to ask it.
H.J. No, but she has put the idea into your head that I am insufferably pushing. Now, hasn't she?

(TINA *makes no answer*)

'Pon my soul, I don't see how any man could be more discreet. Is there any reason why respectable, intelligent people, living under the same roof, should not occasionally pass the time of day? Especially when we are from the same country and share at least some of the same tastes. For, like you, I'm intensely fond of Venice.
TINA. I'm not fond of Venice at all. I would like to be—oh, far away.
H.J. Has she always held you back so?
TINA. I told you she keeps telling me to go out more.
H.J. That's only because she knows you won't leave her now. No, I meant in the past.
TINA. Oh, you mean in the old days?
H.J. Yes. What was it like, your life, in the old days?
TINA. You have travelled a lot and seen the great world. You might not think our life could ever have been up to much. But it was! When we first came to Venice ...

H.J. (*eagerly*) When was that?
TINA. Oh, years ago.
H.J. (*pressing*) Don't you remember the year?
TINA. What does it matter? Then, it was like heaven. You can't imagine what life here was like then. (*From her tone it would seem that she is about to say she knew Marco Polo, or something equally fantastic*) Fancy! Then—there was never a week when we didn't have some visitor or didn't make some pleasant *passeggio* in the town. We saw all the curiosities. We even went across to the lido—in a boat.
H.J. In a boat? Fancy!
TINA. Once we took a cold collation with us. We spread it out on the grass . . .
H.J. Just the two of you? (*He takes a notebook from his inside pocket, and holding it well out of Tina's sight, makes some notes*)
TINA. Oh, no. There were many folk we used to know then, very nice ones, too—the Cavaliere Bombicci, the Countess Altemura. And then there were the Goldies, and our friend from Philadelphia, Mrs Stock-Stock . . .
H.J. (*writing the name in his book*) Philadelphia.
TINA (*her face clouding*) We loved her dearly. But she is dead and gone, poor dear.

(H.J. *crosses the name out in his book*)

But I am afraid that's the case with many of our kind circle, though there are a few left, which is a wonder considering how we have had to neglect them. But the ladies are all getting old now, and even the gentlemen aren't getting any younger. Except the doctor. He never seems to change. He's very clever. He has given up his practice years ago, but he still comes as a friend. You ought to ask him about your heart, he wouldn't mind.
H.J. Thank you, but I have an excellent doctor.
TINA. Then there's the Lawyer Pochintesta. He writes beautiful poems. He once wrote one to my aunt.
H.J. I should like to meet him. Has he called lately?
TINA. Oh, no, they all come only about once a year, usually at New Year, the *capo d'anno*. Auntie used to make them all little presents in the old days. She and I together. Paper lampshades, mats for the wine, mittens for the winter . . .
H.J. I suspect you made most of them.
TINA. But there aren't many presents nowadays. Auntie lost interest a long time ago and—I can't think what to make. (*She pauses*) But sometimes one or other of our friends turns up. (*She looks at him*) You are looking quite sad. (*She rises and takes a step towards him*) Are you in pain again?
H.J. I was only wishing that I had known you both in those far-off days.

(ASSUNTA *enters up the stairs* R *carrying a tray of tea*)

TINA (*crossing to the landing and taking the tray from Assunta*) I
will take it in.

H.J. (*rising and crossing to* C) Must you go? She said she didn't
wish for tea.

TINA. I must see how she is. She often changes her mind.

(ASSUNTA *exits down the stairs* R. TINA *moves towards the doors
up* C, *but* H.J. *intercepts her*)

H.J. I wish she'd change her mind about me.

TINA. (*turning.away up* RC) Oh, you! I don't believe you.

H.J. (*moving to* L *of her*) Why don't you believe me?

TINA. Perhaps because I don't understand you.

H.J. Surely, that is just the sort of occasion to have faith.

TINA (*lingering*) Thank you for the flowers. Don't read or study
late tonight. Get a good sleep.

H.J. (*crossing to the french windows*) I don't read at night in the
summer. The lamplight brings in the animals.

TINA (*moving* C; *lightly*) You might have known that before you
came.

H.J. (*boldly*) I did know it.

TINA. Do you work at night in winter?

H.J. (*moving to* L *of the couch*) I read a good deal. Sometimes I
read myself to sleep. It's a bad habit.

(TINA *moves to the doors up* C *and tries to balance the tray on one
arm in order to open the door*)

TINA. We never tried. I always fall asleep. (*She has her hand on
the door knob*)

H.J. (*making a desperate bid*) I like then to read some great poet.
In nine cases out of ten it's from the works of Jeffrey Aspern.

(TINA *turns to face* H.J., *leaving the door unopened*)

TINA (*quietly*) Oh, we read *him*.

H.J. He is my poet of poets. I know him almost by heart.

TINA (*moving towards* H.J.) Oh, that's nothing! My aunt used
to know him as a—a visitor.

H.J. Indeed?

TINA (*standing up* R *of the couch*) He used to call on her and take
her out.

H.J. But, my dear Miss Tina, he died ages ago.

TINA. She was born ages ago.

(*There is a pause. They come close to each other*)

H.J. (*turning to her*) How odd that I didn't know all this. I
would so like to ask her about him.

TINA. You should have come twenty years ago. She still talked
about him then.

H.J. What did she say?

TINA. I don't know—that he liked her immensely.
H.J. Did she like him?
TINA. She said he was a god.

(*There is a pause.* TINA *looks straight ahead*)

H.J. Has she a portrait of him? They're distressingly rare.

(TINA *does not answer*)

Surely you'd know if she had? It would be on the wall somewhere in a place of honour. Unless, of course, she keeps it locked up.

(TINA *is shaking nervously. This causes* H.J. *to take her wrists to steady her*)

My dear Miss Tina, whatever is the matter?
TINA (*looking H.J. in the face*) Do you write? Do you write about *him*?
H.J. That's another of your aunt's questions.
TINA. No. But please answer it. *Please answer!*
H.J. (*desperately*) Yes. I've written about him and I'm looking for more material. In heaven's name have you got any?

(TINA *looks at H.J. for several seconds, then down at his hands which are holding her arms*)

TINA. Please let me go.

(H.J. *releases* TINA *who moves to the doors up* c)

(*She looks back at him in quiet horror*) Santo Dio!

TINA *exits hurriedly with the tray up* c *as the* LIGHTS *dim to* BLACK-OUT *and—*

the CURTAIN *falls*

SCENE 2

SCENE—*The same. Three weeks later. Early evening.*

When the CURTAIN *rises, there have been further changes in the room. There is not a single flower, and an empty vase remains on the table* RC. *The "sociable" couch has been replaced by a battered Victorian couch, which is covered with a dust sheet. Behind the couch is an old four-fold leather screen. The pedestal from up* L *is below the left end of the screen, and has an oil lamp on it. The console table down* R *has been removed. The chair from* LC *is below the table* RC. *There is a bundle of rugs on the floor down* L, *in front of the stove. The french windows and shutters are open.* ASSUNTA *enters up the stairs* R, *carrying two rugs and a carpet beater. She crosses, puts one rug on the pile down* L, *then throws the second rug over the bundle, covering it completely.* TINA *enters by the double doors and moves down* LC. *She wears a silk dress, tidy but old-fashioned. She wears a rather fine ring. Her hair is neater and she looks as if she may have washed.*

TINA. Have you beaten them, Assunta?
ASSUNTA. Si, Signora.
TINA. That will do for the moment, Assunta. We'll lay the rugs tomorrow. (*She indicates some brushes on the couch*) Take those.

(ASSUNTA *collects a feather duster and a hand brush from the couch. She retains the carpet beater*)

Now go in and stay with the Padrona—she is all dressed—and make the bed.

(ASSUNTA *exits up* C. TINA *takes the dust sheet from the couch, folds it and places it on the bundle down* L. *She tidies the antimacassars on the couch, then crosses to the landing and looks up the stairs. She returns to the couch and sits. A gondolier is heard singing, on the canal, a long way off.*
H.J. *enters down the stairs* R.
PASQUALE *follows him on.* H.J. *is in full evening dress.* PASQUALE *carries* H.J.*'s cape, hat, white gloves and cane.* TINA *rises.* H.J. *stops in amazement on seeing Tina waiting for him. He bows*)

Oh, you are going out?
H.J. (*coldly*) You have guessed correctly. Pasquale, tell the gondolier to wait.

(PASQUALE *puts the hat with cane on the table on the landing, crosses the landing and exits down the stairs* R)

(*He comes into the room*) I was beginning to think we might not ever bump into one another again, before I leave. It is nearly three weeks since I last had the pleasure.
TINA (*moving* C) You have to leave Venice?
H.J. No, but my doctor is of the opinion that for me to climb sixty-three steps several times a day is, in his phrase, "*molto pericoloso*".
TINA. That's one thing I was waiting to ask you about.
H.J. Indeed?
TINA. You suggested that if you had the use of the sala and . . .
H.J. I did. But that was nearly three weeks ago. It took me two weeks before I realized that I should no more get an answer to that question than to the others I put to you at the same time. You thought me impertinent. Perhaps I was. (*He moves down* R *of the table* RC) Forgive me.
TINA. No, no.
H.J. You discussed the matter with your aunt?
TINA. About the rooms, yes.
H.J. Well?

TINA. I think it may be all right; she wishes to see you.

H.J. Now?

TINA. Yes, now.

H.J. (*still very cold and dry*) An unexpected honour. But I think I know what she will say: I may have the use of the larger rooms if I pay a much larger rent. (*As he speaks he glances at the door down* R) Isn't that about it?

TINA (*slowly, though she has thought it all out*) You could pay the same, or even a bit less. She would never know. She doesn't count her money.

H.J. (*sincerely*) My dear Miss Tina, I should not have thought you capable of deceit towards anybody, let alone your aunt.

TINA (*turning away down* L) I've thought about it and it seems to me that since the money is for me—it's for me to decide whether it's too much or too little . . . (*The shame of her deceit overcomes her*)

(*There is a pause*)

H.J. (*crossing below the table to* C; *moved*) I could not let you do that. I will pay whatever she asks.

TINA. Oh, no!

H.J. (*crossing to* R *of her*) I will pay what she asks or leave Venice. I am sorry I used the word deceit. You are the soul of honesty. (*He studies her changed appearance*) Permit me to say that is a most charming dress.

TINA. My aunt told me to wear it. It is my best one.

H.J. Now, tell me, did you—repeat to her—the other things I told you that afternoon?

TINA. About Mr Aspern? Do you imagine she would want to see you if I had?

H.J. She may want to keep him to herself. Her object in seeing me may be to tell me so.

TINA (*crossing above H.J. and moving up* C) I must tell her you are here. (*She turns to him*) She won't want to speak of him.

(H.J. *turns to face her*)

Believe me, I have told her nothing.

(TINA, *to avoid further discussion, exits hurriedly up* C, *leaving both doors open.* H.J. *crosses to the landing*)

H.J. (*calling*) Pasquale.

PASQUALE (*off*) Yes, signore?

H.J. Tell the gondolier I am obliged to keep him waiting still. Tell him on no account to go away.

PASQUALE (*off*) Yes, signore.

(H.J. *crosses down* L, *takes his notebook from his pocket, writes in*

*it, replaces it in his pocket then takes up a somewhat arrogant, pro-
prietary stance by the stove. He is determined to fight a battle, if need be.*

TINA *pushes* JULIANA *on up* C. JULIANA *also is dressed differently in that she wears a bright shawl, with metal in it, possibly Indian
work. The shawl glitters oddly against Juliana's nondescript clothes.*

ASSUNTA *follows them on.* TINA *pushes the wheel chair to* C
and stands up R *of it.* H.J. *is determined that this time he will neither
rush things nor allow himself to be rushed. He bows, and stays at a
distance.*

ASSUNTA *exits up* C, *closing the doors behind her*)

JULIANA. You may sit down.

H.J. Thank you. (*But he remains standing. With somewhat elaborate
composure*) It has been extraordinarily hot these last few days. I
hope it has not affected you?

JULIANA. I have been well enough. They say it is a great thing
to be alive.

H.J. (*boldly, but as if carelessly*) As to that, it depends what you
compare it with.

JULIANA. I don't compare. If I did that I should have given up
everything long ago. Were you about to go out?

H.J. I have time to spare. My punctuality is becoming a vice.

JULIANA. What's happened to all the beautiful flowers?

(H.J. *looks idly round the room as if he had only just noticed the
absence of flowers*)

Do you keep them to yourself? It's not a manly taste to make a
bower of your room.

H.J. (*unruffled*) I don't make it into a bower, but there is
nothing unmanly in a love of flowers. (*He circles the couch and stands
up* L *of it, looking out of the windows*) I didn't think you had noticed
them. Or the garden. Have you noticed the garden recently, Miss
Tina?

JULIANA. You must make her see it. Come and fetch her if need
be.

H.J. (*moving below the couch*) It would do you both good to sit
there again from time to time. (*He sits on the right end of the couch*)
There is now plenty of shade in the arbour. And the air at this
time of the evening can be very sweet.

JULIANA (*as if flirting*) Oh, sir, when next I move out of here
it won't be into the air, and any that may be stirring round me
won't be particularly sweet. I've had arbours enough in my time.
But *she*—she's seen nothing.

TINA. Auntie! (*To H.J.*) I told you, she's always telling me to
go out. You see I can do what I like. (*She moves to* L *of the table and
sits facing H.J.*)

JULIANA. Do you pity her? Do you encourage her to pity herself? She's had an easier life than I had at her age.

H.J. Possibly. But no two human beings are the same.
JULIANA (*seizing on the word*) I'm "inhuman", perhaps?
H.J. I didn't say so.
JULIANA. That's what the poets used to call the women in the old days. Don't try that. You won't do as well as they. There's no more poetry in the world—that *I* know of at least. What do you think?
H.J. Well . . .
JULIANA (*cutting him short*) But don't make me bandy words with you. You will make me talk, talk, talk. It isn't good for me.

(*H.J. looks quizzically at Juliana, almost with insolence*)

By the way, what's all this about a weak heart? I suspected as much when I first saw you.
H.J. That is extremely interesting. May I ask why?
JULIANA. You talked some nonsense about "love at first sight". That's either a weak heart or a weak head, or both.

(*H.J. laughs slightly, rises, moves down L and turns to face Juliana*)

H.J. I might have guessed you would know all about conditions of the heart.
JULIANA. What does that mean?
H.J. (*who has gone too far*) Nothing. I am so very happy to think you will permit me to see you again.
JULIANA. Is it so very necessary to your happiness?
H.J. It diverts me more than I can say.

(*The antagonism between the two has now reached the degree of a duel*)

JULIANA (*acidly*) You're wonderfully civil. Don't you know civility almost kills me?
TINA. Auntie!
H.J. (*with a step towards Juliana*) How can I believe that, when I see you more animated, more brilliant than ever?
TINA. That's very true, Auntie. I think it does you good.
JULIANA (*turning on her, ready to fire on friend or foe alike*) Isn't it touching, the solicitude we all have for each other? (*To H.J.*) If you think me brilliant today you don't know what you're talking about. I don't suppose you've ever seen an agreeable woman. What do you people know about good society. Don't try to pay me compliments. I have been spoiled. (*She beckons H.J. to her*)

(H.J. *moves to* L *of Juliana*)

Do you remember, the day I saw you about the rooms, that you offered me the use of your gondola?
H.J. Of course. Do you wish to avail yourself of the offer at last?

JULIANA. Why don't you take the girl out in it and show her the place.

TINA. Oh, dear Aunt! I know all about the place.

JULIANA. Do you? Well then, go with him and explain. Haven't we heard there have been all sorts of changes?

(H.J. *crosses down* L *and turns to Juliana*)

You ought to see them, and at your age—and I don't mean because you're so "young"—you ought to take the chances that offer. You're old enough, my dear; and the gentleman won't hurt you. He'll show you the famous sunsets, if they still go on. Do they go on? The sun set for me long ago. Go on. I shan't miss you.

TINA (*rising and moving to* R *of Juliana*) But, Auntie . . .

JULIANA. You think you're too important. Take her to the Piazza. It used to be very pretty. Oh, what have they done with that funny old church? Show her the shops. Lend her some money. You can deduct it from the rent.

(*There is a short pause*)

Well, why don't you say something?

TINA. Auntie, it's not very easy for Mr Jessamine to . . .

H.J. If Miss Tina will do me the honour to . . .

JULIANA. Yes, yes, yes, she'll do you the honour. You'd better go *now*.

TINA. Mr Jessamine may have an appointment.

JULIANA. Have you? Have you an appointment?

H.J. I have two, but I shall be missed at neither, I trust.

JULIANA. Then that's settled. Go on, take him out. Entertain him and he'll probably want to stay here another six months.

H.J. I'm a poor devil from Grub Street who lives from day to day. How can I afford to take Palazzos by the half year?

JULIANA. If you write books, don't you sell them? What do you write about?

H.J. About other people's books. (*Cautiously*) I'm a critic, an historian, in a small way.

JULIANA. What other people?

H.J. Oh, better ones than myself. The great writers, mainly.

JULIANA. And what do you say about them?

H.J. (*after a pause; with great daring*) I say they sometimes attached themselves to very clever women.

JULIANA. In other words, you rake up the past. I like the past, but I don't like scandal-mongers. *Ces colporteurs de médisances!* The truth is God's, not man's. How can we judge it?

H.J. (*moving to* L *of Juliana*) But if we give up trying, how will the measure of their work be reckoned?

JULIANA. Not by their lives. Some of the greatest of them were cheats and wastrels. Have you ever seen a mortal god? No, of course you haven't, or you wouldn't talk of reckoning. You would merely watch and wonder. And be silent.

H.J. (*leaning towards Juliana*) I was speaking of the work, not the man.

(JULIANA *now draws out from the folds of her purple shawl a package wrapped in a velvet bag*)

JULIANA. Do you know anything about curiosities? The gimcracks people pay so much for today? Do you know the kind of price they bring?

H.J. That depends on the gimcrack and the fashion.

(JULIANA *takes a small portrait from the bag*)

JULIANA. What would an *amateur* give me for that?

H.J. Permit me? (*He picks up the portrait from Juliana's lap. We can guess from his controlled agitation whose portrait it is. He gazes at it for a second or two*) What a striking face! (*He moves below the right end of the couch*) Who is it?

JULIANA. He's an old friend of mine. The world goes fast and one generation forgets another. It's a question of fashion, as you say. He was all the fashion when I was young.

(H.J. *looks sharply at Tina and then at the portrait*)

Tina knows a song of his. It's a translation from the Italian. It's an old tune. I taught it her myself. Sing it, Tina.

TINA. It's time you were in bed.

JULIANA (*disregarding her*) When she was a young girl she used to come down and sing to the guests at parties. She would stand here under the chandelier. She was always a plain child but her voice used to be very sweet. Tina, sing *The Green Hussars*!

TINA. Auntie!

JULIANA. Don't argue with me. It's probably the last time you'll be asked to sing by me——

TINA. It's time you went to bed.

JULIANA. —or by anyone else, for that matter.

(TINA *is troubled, but the prospect of her evening out has given her a little confidence*)

H.J. Yes, my dear Miss Tina, please sing.

TINA (*crossing above the wheel chair and facing H.J.*) I don't know if I can remember the words.

H.J. (*sitting on the right end of the couch*) Please try.

(*That is enough for* TINA. *She composes herself to sing*)

TINA (*to Juliana*) *The Green Hussars* always used to upset you a bit.

JULIANA. Nothing "upsets" me now.

(TINA *sings as well as she can. Her confidence and voice grow as she goes on. H.J. sits listening and looks now at the two women, now at the portrait on his knees*)

TINA (*singing*)
Down fall the feathers of his bottle-green shako
Down fall the limbs of my lily-white boy
Near sounds the whinny of a riderless charger,
Far are the trumpeters and gone my joy.

Curly his hair it was, his mouth sweet as apple
Hard were his limbs and his eye bright as day
So light and fleet he was, so slender and supple
Only a boy he was, my friends would say.

Few were the times we met, furtive and seldom
Few were the hours I lay locked in his arm
But there content I'd be, my body his kingdom
No foe could fright him there, no wars alarm.

Where are the Green Hussars who left the town smiling?
Where are the cheers of that bright summer morn?
What cheer is comfort to a woman who's wailing?
What fellow fathers now my child unborn?

(*After the song, there is a pause. H.J., moved, rises, takes Tina's hand and kisses it. TINA moves up R of the wheel chair*)

H.J. Thank you. (*He looks at the portrait*) You say the song was written by this man? Who was he? Should I know him?

JULIANA. It's only a person who would know for himself who would give me my price. (*She makes a compelling movement with her arms for him to restore the picture to her*)

H.J. I have an idea. (*He moves to L of Juliana and hands her the portrait*) If you would entrust me with it for twenty-four hours I could ask expert advice on it. I should like to have it myself, but . . .

(JULIANA *catches her breath sharply as she puts the portrait under her shawl. H.J. moves down L and turns to face Juliana*)

JULIANA. You'd buy the likeness of someone you don't know by an artist of no reputation?

H.J. The artist may have no reputation, but it's wonderfully well-painted.

JULIANA. It's lucky you thought of saying that. The artist was my father.

H.J. (*moving to L of Juliana*) Well, in that event, remember me as a possible purchaser. Have you any idea of its value?

JULIANA. I know the least I would take. I want to know the most I could get.
H.J. And what is the least?
JULIANA. A thousand pounds.
TINA. Oh, Lord!

(H.J. *crosses down* R. *His excitement, so long controlled, causes him to begin to laugh.*
PASQUALE *enters up the stairs* R *and waits on the landing. He holds H.J.'s cloak and gloves.* JULIANA's *face trembles with anger at H.J.'s laughter*)

H.J. I haven't a thousand pounds. And I very much doubt if anyone would . . . (*He stops as he sees Juliana's face. Sincerely*) I am most dreadfully sorry. Look, I know the very man who will tell you the least and the most it is worth. May I bring him to see you tomorrow?
JULIANA. You all want to *see* me. And I want to *watch you*. I want to watch this clever gentleman.
TINA (*moving to* R *of Juliana*) Don't get so excited. It isn't good for you. (*To H.J.*) She can be horribly imprudent. (*To Juliana*) If I go out, promise you won't start dragging yourself round the house as soon as my back is turned. (*To H.J.*) I don't know how she does it. Assunta says she doesn't help her.
JULIANA. Never you mind how I do what I do. I've always got most things done I've wanted, thank God. People have humoured me.
H.J. (*with a smile*) You mean they've obeyed you.

(*It is an imprudent remark.* JULIANA *pauses and then gets very excited again*)

JULIANA. Well! Whatever it is—when they like me.
TINA. You're agitating her dreadfully.

(*This agitates* JULIANA *even more.* H.J. *turns and beckons to* PASQUALE *who comes forward, assists* H.J. *into his cloak and gives him his white kid gloves while* JULIANA *chatters on.* TINA *starts to move the wheel chair. She pushes it down* C *and then draws it backwards down* LC)

JULIANA. "Excited"! "Agitated"! "Imprudent"! Your generation doesn't know how to live. I learnt to live while I was still young and I haven't quite lost the knack. I'll live until I'm dead and that's more than most of you can say. (*To Pasquale*) Here! You fellow. Wheel me in.

(PASQUALE *crosses and takes the wheel chair from* TINA *who moves down* L)

TINA. But, Auntie, he doesn't know the rooms.
JULIANA. Well, he can find out, can't he?

(PASQUALE *moves the wheel chair towards the double doors*)

Run along, the two of you. (*She arrests Pasquale with a gesture. To H.J.*) You may use this room, if you desire it, and the rooms beyond. (*She points to the door down* R) The whole wing, if you wish it. You told Miss Tina that your present rooms weren't worth the money, it seems.

H.J. Well, are they?

JULIANA. No, but it's the sum I need. I can't take less. Take it or leave it.

(H.J. *hesitates*)

H.J. Well . . .

JULIANA. You may tap on my door, sir, when the two of you come back.

H.J. (*astounded*) I take it.

JULIANA. You take it? Very well, then, there's no need to tap on my door, is there? (*She chuckles. To Pasquale*) Avanti!

(ASSUNTA *enters up* C *carrying two sheets.*
    PASQUALE *wheels* JULIANA *off up* C.
    ASSUNTA *closes the double doors, then crosses to the landing and exits down the stairs* R)

H.J. (*crossing to* C; *quietly and with a watchful eye on Assunta as she goes*) Are you quite sure you did not mention that other little matter to Miss Bordereau?

TINA. About Mr Aspern? Of course I'm sure. It's no "little matter" to her.

H.J. It's hard to believe that she is unaware of my interest in him.

TINA. Why?

H.J. She is laughing at me. "What do you people know of good society," she says. If the manners of her age were so fine— which I venture to doubt—she might give us a taste of their quality.

TINA. I wish you would not speak of her as if she were something in a book.

(PASQUALE, *unseen by* TINA, *enters silently up* C *and closes the doors behind him*)

H.J. (*seeing Pasquale*) When was it you last went on the water, did you say?

TINA (*turning to face H.J.*) I didn't say.

H.J. (*surreptitiously indicating Pasquale's presence to her*) Pasquale, I seem to have left my gold match-case on my dressing-table.

PASQUALE. Very good, Signore.

(PASQUALE *moves to the landing and exits up the stairs*)

H.J. (*raising his voice until Pasquale is out of carshot*) I thought we might take a considerable *giro* before going to the Piazza. What do you think?

TINA. Oh, no. Let us, please, go straight to the Piazza. That's what I want to see.

H.J. (*crossing to Tina*) Then we will disembark straightway at the Piazzetta and take a turn round the great square before taking a table at *Florians?*

TINA. Oh, *Florians*, yes! And can I buy an ice?

H.J. That is one of Miss Bordereau's suggestions most calculated to offend me. *Buy* an ice, indeed.

TINA. You're wrong to think she wishes to offend you. She's afraid you'll go.

H.J. Indeed?

TINA. She's afraid you've not been happy.

H.J. She wants to make me happier?

TINA. She wants you not to go.

H.J. (*bluntly*) You mean on account of the rent? I understand that plainly enough. But don't you think she ought to fix the sum you need, so that I may know how long to stay before it's made up?

(TINA *turns away.* PASQUALE *enters part way down the stairs and stands, listening*)

TINA (*after a moment's thought*) No. I think you should give up your—reasons, and go away altogether.

H.J. It's not so easy to give up my reasons.

TINA (*turning to him; in a sudden outburst of anguish*) She would never consent to what you want. She has been asked—written to—it makes her fearfully angry. She hates publishers.

H.J. Then she has papers of value?

TINA. She has *everything.*

(H.J. *comforts Tina by holding her by the shoulders*)

H.J. Please, dear Miss Tina, don't cry. We are going for a trip in a gondola; we mustn't cry in a gondola, must we?

TINA (*smiling a little*) Oh no, that would never do.

H.J. We have done nothing wrong in discussing things. Now, dry your eyes and tell me that *you* trust me. Eh? Then we'll go out and have a jolly evening.

TINA. I'd like to.

H.J. You'd like to trust me?

TINA. And have a jolly evening.

(PASQUALE *comes on to the landing, picks up H.J.'s opera hat and cane, and moves down* C. *He clears his throat to attract attention.* H.J. *crosses to* PASQUALE *who hands him his match-case, opera hat and cane*)

H.J. Thank you, Pasquale.

(PASQUALE *exits down the stairs* R)

(*To Tina*) Come then. Let us go, before the light fades. But first, say you forgive me for being importunate.

(TINA, *who has recovered like a child, crosses to H.J.*)

TINA. Oh, I do understand how important it is to you.

H.J. Do you? Then you'll help me?

(TINA *looks at him*)

(*He takes her by the shoulders*) My dear Miss Tina, you will help me, won't you?

TINA. I'll do *what I can* to help you.

H.J. *releases* TINA, *offers his arm, and they go on to the landing as the* LIGHTS *dim to* BLACK-OUT *and—*

the CURTAIN *falls*

SCENE 3

SCENE--*The same. Later that evening.*

When the CURTAIN *rises, it is just before midnight. The room is empty and very faint moonlight is to be seen through the shutters. A lamp is burning fairly brightly on the landing table and another lamp, on the pedestal* L, *gives a dim glow. The general appearance of the room is the same as at the end of the previous scene, but although the bundle on the floor near the stove looks the same, the top rug and the dust sheet on it now cover a green trunk instead of the rugs previously under it. The voices and footsteps of* TINA *and* H.J. *are heard ascending the stairs* R. *They sound relaxed and happy, though* H.J.*'s cheerfulness has an ironic ring.*

TINA (*off*) My aunt says that the gentlemen of today are not like the cavaliere of yesterday.

H.J. (*off*) And what do you say?

(H.J. *and* TINA *enter on the landing.* TINA *is wearing* H.J.*'s cloak and has a bunch of violets he has bought her.* H.J. *is smoking a cigar and carrying a small hand oil lamp*)

TINA. I say a gentleman—is a gentleman.

H.J. A simple truth, most charmingly expressed.

TINA (*moving up* RC *and turning to him*) Of course, I don't know much about gentlemen.

H.J. (*coming into the room*) Please do not qualify. You will spoil it.

TINA. I was only going to say—

H.J. (*laughing*) Please!

TINA. —that you are a very strange gentleman.

H.J. Ah!

TINA. Until this evening I always thought—oh, forgive me, please, saying this—I always thought—you seemed to talk more than you thought. (*She giggles*) Do you see what I mean? (*She crosses to* LC)

(H.J. *places his lamp on the table up* RC)

Oh, look, Assunta has put a light in your room. (*She goes to the lamp* L *and turns it up*)

H.J. (*moving below the right end of the couch*) So it's my room now, eh?

TINA. We're going to lay the rugs tomorrow. I know we weren't going to talk about this again tonight . . .

(H.J. *starts to interrupt*)

No, I remember our promises. But—please tell me—what first made you interested in Mr Aspern?

(H.J. *relights his cigar and gestures to Tina to sit.* TINA *sits on the couch at the left end*)

H.J. (*sitting* R *of Tina on the couch*) What I originally prized him for was that at a time when our America was crude and provincial, when the famous "atmosphere" it was supposed to lack was not even missed; when literature was lonely and art an unknown quantity, he had found means to live and write like one of the first; that is why your aunt and I agree about one thing: he was a god. But she has no right to keep her god to herself. I do assure you, Miss Tina, when all his poems and everything is published, to us Americans, he will be our morning star; he will hang high in the heavens of our literature for all the world to see. He will be the light by which we walk. Do you understand? Or are you thinking once more that I am talking too much?

TINA. I understand, and you talk beautifully.

H.J. Tell me, if you have not told your aunt what I confessed to you three weeks ago, may she not perhaps have guessed it?

TINA. I don't know. She's very suspicious.

H.J. Why?

TINA. It's on account of something—years ago, before I was born. Some tragedy.

H.J. I wonder what that might be?

TINA. Oh, she has never told me.

H.J. Not—something to which Mr Aspern's letter and papers and things have reference?

TINA (*as if this were a good suggestion*) Oh, I daresay. I've never looked at them.

H.J. Then how do you know what they are?

TINA. I've seen them when she had them out from the trunk she keeps under her bed.

H.J. Is that often?

TINA. Not now. But she's still fond of them.

H.J. In spite of their being compromising?

TINA. Compromising?

H.J. I mean: containing painful memories? Some things affecting her reputation?

TINA. Do you mean she ever did something bad?

H.J. Even if she did, it was in another age, another world. But she might still wish to destroy them.

TINA. But she *loves* them.

H.J. Before she goes, I mean.

TINA (*on the verge of tears*) Perhaps—then—when she's sure of going—she will.

(*There is a pause*)

H.J. That is what we must prevent. (*He rises*) You must get them away from her.

(TINA *rises, simply appalled*)

TINA (*without irony*) And give them to you?

H.J. Simply to look at. To copy. Not for me. For posterity. Surely you trust me, don't you?

TINA. Yes, I trust you, but she trusts me. (*She takes her handkerchief from her bag, and weeps*)

H.J. (*after a pause*) Yes. Then perhaps we shall both sleep tonight with less troubled minds; you because you feel you can trust me more, I because I have your promise that you will help me. I think we should now say good night. (*He glances at his watch*)

(TINA *stands looking at him*)

What do you say, Miss Tina?

TINA. I say this has been—one of the most beautiful evenings of my life.

(H.J. *crosses to the table up* R, *picks up his lamp, then goes on to the landing and turns.* TINA *goes to the lamp on the pedestal* L., *turns it down, then crosses towards the landing*)

H.J. Good night.

TINA. Good night, and thank you.

(H.J. *smiles and exits up the stairs with his lamp.* TINA *crosses towards the stove. As she passes the end of the couch something on the floor catches her eye and she picks it up. It is Juliana's eye shade. For a moment* TINA *stands in alarm then she exits swiftly by the doors up* C, *leaving them open. We hear her strange sob of panic. She hurries back*

*into the sala and makes for the landing, calling first for Juliana, then
for Assunta and then* "*Mr Jessamine*".
H.J. *enters down the stairs*)

H.J. Whatever is the matter, my dear?
Tina. I can't find her. I can't find Miss Bordereau.
H.J. Don't be alarmed, she must be somewhere.

(Assunta, *in her nightgown and with her hair unbraided, appears
on the landing, and, muttering to herself crosses towards the french
windows, above the screen*)

(*He crosses to* c, *looking after Assunta*) Look! (*He points to what he
sees behind the screen*) How did she get there?

(Assunta *wheels* Juliana *in her wheel chair from behind the
screen to* c. Juliana *is in her nightgown and peignoire. A wisp of lace
covers the top of her almost bald head. A white shawl is on her lap.
Her eyes are open but* "*their sense is shut*". *We are not sure, for a
moment, whether this figure, seemingly carved in ivory, is dead or alive.*
Tina *crosses to the lamp* l *and turns it up.* H.J. *puts his lamp on the
table* RC *and goes down* R)

Tina. Auntie! Oh, goodness gracious, you gave us quite a
fright. What are you sitting out here for?

(H.J. *looks closely at Juliana*)

(*She chatters on*) We had a wonderful dinner at *Florians*. I had an
ice and Mr Jessamine gave me these violets. Look!

(H.J. *makes a gesture to* Tina, *who stops abruptly and looks at
Juliana.* Assunta *moves towards the landing, then stops and turns.
The three of them stand rooted in terror, gazing at* Juliana. *Then the
old lady's eyelids flutter and she starts to speak.* Tina *moves to* l *of
the wheel chair*)

Juliana. They don't have to light all the candles—they'll set
the place on fire—it's too hot as it is. (*She throws off the white shawl
which covers her knees*)

(Tina *replaces the shawl over Juliana's knees*)

What's that they're playing? Who told them they could start the
quadrille—keep time—*a tempo, a tempo*—you'd think they were
dancing a dirge—I'm giddy.

(Assunta *kneels* R *of the wheel chair*)

Tina. Auntie! It's just a bad dream.
Juliana. Who's that he's dancing with? She wasn't invited.
How dare he bring her here? Go and tell her, with the utmost
politeness of course, that if she comes near me I shall spit in her
face—tell her that—go on—tell her.

TINA. There, there, hush, Auntie.

H.J. (*whispering incisively*) No! No! (*He moves below the table* RC) Let her go on. Let her talk.

TINA. How can you? Can't you see she's ill?

H.J. *Let her talk!*

(PASQUALE *enters down the stairs and stands on the landing, watching*)

JULIANA. Tina—Tina—Tina, my darling, come close to me. (*In her delirium she gropes for the child Tina*) Come close to the only one that loves you.

(JULIANA *beats aside* TINA, *who is standing by her, and instead caresses the head of* ASSUNTA, *who is kneeling by her, stroking the white shawl round her legs.* ASSUNTA *starts to wail quietly.* TINA *is dumb with horror*)

Do you see that fair woman over there? Never trust a fair Italian woman—they're all cheats and liars. You're all mine—you're all of his I've got—she gave you up, remember that. "Nessun maggior dolore—nella miseria." " There is no greater sorrow than to remember, in misery, a time of happiness."

(JULIANA *rises to her feet.* TINA *and* ASSUNTA *support her*)

Basta—Basta—stop the music! The party is over—and as for you, Madame—I am not narrow-minded—but I could never so far forget myself as to ask my friends to meet the daughter—of a whore. (*She summons up all her energy and spits on the ground in front of her, then she collapses*)

TINA. Assunta!

(ASSUNTA *and* TINA *help* JULIANA *into her chair.* PASQUALE *moves to the doors up* C, *opens the doors wide and makes sure the passage is clear. He then stands* R *of the double doors.* TINA *wheels* JULIANA *off up* C. ASSUNTA *follows them off.* H.J. *follows the wheel chair up* C, *then returns and sits* R *of the table* RC. PASQUALE *closes the double doors.* H.J. *pulls out his notebook and begins to scribble in it what he can remember of what Juliana has said*)

PASQUALE (*moving up* L *of the table*) My lord! It is important for you? The picture?

(H.J. *is too occupied to be aware of anything more than Pasquale's presence*)

When the old lady recovers she will want to put it back in the green trunk.

H.J. (*looking up sharply*) A *green* trunk? What do you know about a trunk?

PASQUALE. When I wheeled Miss Bordereau through the parlour into her bedroom, I happened to see it. It was sticking out from under the bed.

H.J. Was it open?
PASQUALE. Yes.
H.J. (*rising and standing up* R *of the table*) Did you *happen* to see what was in it?
PASQUALE. Many papers. Letters, I think. Tied up in ribbons.

(TINA *enters up* C. H.J. *motions to* PASQUALE *to keep silent and he crosses to* LC)

TINA (*moving down* RC) Pasquale, you know where the doctor lives, don't you? Please fetch him at once. (*To H.J.*) He lives only three doors away.
PASQUALE. May I go, signore?
H.J. Of course. Hurry!

(PASQUALE *crosses above Tina to the landing*)

(*He moves up* L *of the table*) Hurry back.

(PASQUALE *exits hurriedly down the stairs* R)

TINA (*moving up* R *of the table and calling after Pasquale*) You may leave the door open. (*To H.J.*) She's had one of her attacks.
H.J. Don't worry. She won't go yet.
TINA. If she does, it will be because of you.
H.J. What have I done?
TINA. You made her angry.
H.J. Is she conscious? May I see her for a moment? No. If I make her angry, I suppose she should be spared the sight of me. Miss Tina, I feel very guilty. Do you remember, some months ago, receiving a letter from America? From a publisher? You answered it yourself.
TINA. Yes.
H.J. I was a party to that letter.
TINA. You were?
H.J. Yes, I feel very guilty. I have sailed under false colours. But now you shall know the truth. There's nothing wrong with my heart. I don't like gardens and flowers any more than the next man. Even my name is not my own. My sole reason for being in Venice this Summer is to see what she may have of Jeffrey Aspern's papers. That, believe me, believe me, is the whole truth.
TINA. What is your name?
H.J. Jarvis. Henry Jarvis.
TINA (*amazed*) Gracious! (*She pauses*) I like your own name best. I feel I can trust you better as Mr Jarvis.
H.J. Then you will look and see *what* is in that trunk?
TINA. But the trunk isn't there.
H.J. How do you know?
TINA. I saw just now. She must have moved it.

H.J. (*crossing up* L *and looking at the double doors*) How could she have done that? Could Assunta have helped her?

(Assunta *enters up* c)

Tina (*moving to* R *of Assunta*) Well?
Assunta. She is sleeping. Breathing much better. But hands are very cold.
Tina. Go down and boil some water to fill a hot-water bottle.

(Assunta *crosses to the landing.* Tina *turns and follows her.* H.J. *signals to Tina to ask Assunta about the trunk*)

Assunta! Where has my aunt put her old trunk?
Assunta. Please?
Tina. Il baule? Where is it?

(Assunta *looks innocently bewildered*)

You know the one I mean. Never mind. Boil the water, Assunta.

(Assunta *exits down the stairs* R)

(*She turns to H.J.*) She doesn't know.

(H.J. *suddenly strides towards the stove, feels it, kneels on the pile of rugs and looks inside the stove*)

(*She crosses to H.J.*) What are you doing?
H.J. (*rising, turning and wiping his hands with his handkerchief*) Well, if she's capable of moving the trunk herself she may even have burnt them.
Tina. I don't see how she could have done that. Not all by herself.

(Pasquale *enters swiftly up the stairs* R)

Pasquale (*a little out of breath*) Signorina, the dottore is out. The avvocato's wife is having a baby.
Tina (*crossing up* RC) Signora Pochintesta?

(Pasquale *nods*)

But that's way over on the Giudecca. (*She thinks for a moment then turns and moves towards the double doors*) Wait. (*She stops and turns*) There is another doctor lives by San Polo's. Do you know him?
Pasquale. No, signorina. Sorry.
H.J. (*moving towards Tina*) Can I help?
Tina (*moving down* LC) Lend me your cloak again. I will go.

(H.J. *picks up his cloak from the couch and puts it around Tina's shoulders*)

Pasquale, please help Assunta with the hot-water bottles. Tell her to sit by my aunt. I'll leave the door open.

(TINA *crosses and exits hurriedly down the stairs* R. PASQUALE *does not go, but watches* H.J. *who goes to the screen behind the couch, moves it a little, then opens the downstage shutter of the french windows and goes out on to the balcony for a moment. He re-enters and moves up* C)

H.J. Go and help Assunta, Pasquale.

PASQUALE. Will your lordship return to England soon?

H.J. When I go, I shall be going to America.

PASQUALE (*moving to* R *of H.J.*) Perhaps his lordship will take Pasquale with him to America?

H.J. Pasquale, how many times must I tell you: I am *not a lord.*

PASQUALE. His Lordship's secret is safe with me. I have heard of the scandal your brother caused in Venice last year. His letters—you wish to save him from blackmail.

(H.J., *extremely irritated, crosses below the table to* R, *turns and moves down* R *of the table*)

H.J. I haven't the least idea what you are talking about.

PASQUALE (*moving down* L) I could help you find the letters, my lord. But if I did, it would be very difficult for me to stay in Venice. If your lordship needed me in America, it would be easier.

H.J. You're a cool one to talk of blackmail, I must say. We'll talk about this tomorrow. It's no good looking tonight. Go to bed. In any case, the trunk has disappeared.

PASQUALE. No, my lord.

H.J. (*crossing below the table to* C *and facing up stage*) I tell you it's gone. Miss Tina has told me so.

PASQUALE *moves swiftly to the pile in front of the stove, pulls aside the top rug and reveals the green trunk. He pulls the trunk away from the stove*)

(*The sound causes him to turn*) Did *you* put that there?

PASQUALE. Yes, my lord. When you and the lady were out.

H.J. That was very wrong of you, Pasquale. Is it unlocked?

PASQUALE. Yes, my lord. (*He runs below H.J. across to the landing*) I think it would be better if I keep Assunta in the kitchen. For five minutes.

(PASQUALE *exits down the stairs* R. H.J., *left alone, goes to the trunk and kneels beside it. He feverishly pulls at the old straps which bind it. One of these breaks. The door up* C *opens silently.*
    JULIANA *enters slowly up* C *and blinks in the light. Leaning against the lintel she looks around and soon her attention is caught by the kneeling figure of H.J. She advances slowly and very unsteadily, groping for something on which to steady herself. H.J. is so busy, trying to undo the straps, that he is oblivious to any other sound. Sud-*

denly he hears Juliana *gasp as she realizes what is happening, and turns and sees her*)

Juliana (*hissing with passion and fury*) You publishing scoundrel!
H.J. (*rising*) No! No!

(Juliana *starts to retreat from* H.J. *waving him off with her hands. Her flailing arms cause her to lose balance and she falls unconscious to the ground. As she falls* H.J. *gives a despairing cry*)

Miss Bordereau!

H.J. *kneels beside Juliana as—-*

the Curtain *falls*

ACT III

SCENE—*The same. Twelve days later. Afternoon.*

The sala presents a strange appearance. Every inch that does not block the to and fro from the various doors and entrances is covered with things to be sold. As a "still life" it presents "the last day in the old home". Down R there is a pile of plates and a vase. Above the door down R there is a bundle of rugs, covered by a rug to look like the covered trunk. On top there is a tailor's basket dummy, a gondolier's hat and some napkins. Beside the bundle are various vases. The "sociable" couch is down RC, covered by a dust sheet. On it there is a pile of napkins. Down L of the "sociable" there is an old parrot cage of rather remarkable proportions with faded gilded columns, a wooden bucket, a hand brush and a duster. Four oil lamps stand on the landing table, beside which is Tina's umbrella. There is a feather duster on the console table up RC and two oil paintings lean against it. Down L, above the stove is a crumpled soft rug, a pile of books and a pile of plates. A rolled rug lies beside the downstage side of the french windows. The Victorian couch is down LC. On the right end of it stands the green trunk, and the portrait in the velvet bag, both covered by a dust sheet to look like a bundle of odds and ends. In the trunk there is a shako, a pair of uniform trousers and some papers tied with faded ribbons. On the left end of the couch is a turned-up console table with a pile of books. A console table, up-turned, is L of the couch. The leather screen is on its side leaning against the back of the couch. The circular table is up R of the couch LC. On it there is a large brown trunk, partly covered by a dust sheet, and some letters and newspapers by post. Two stacked chairs with a pile of books and a bronze statue are R of the table. A pedestal table with an upturned chair and a pile of books on it are L of the table. Up L there is a pedestal, the gilt screen and two stacked chairs with a pile of books. L of the double doors there are four large vases, and a large garden vase containing some parasols, umbrellas and a carpet beater.

When the CURTAIN rises, *the light is rather lowering and as if in anticipation of a storm. Distant thunder is heard from time to time. The shutters of the french windows are open and one of them swings idly in the breeze from time to time, making a sharp sound as it hits against the wall. The leaves of the vine and the magnolia are quivering.* ASSUNTA *is down RC, cleaning out the parrot cage, sweeping the sand and feathers, etc. into a bucket. She does this noisily, in the way that Italian domestics seem to love making a noise when they are working.* PASQUALE *is pacing about, twiddling the brim of his hat and watching Assunta in a rather bored and distracted manner. He moves down C, goes up C, moves to the french windows, then stands up L of the table LC and sorts out the mail.*

PASQUALE. This is today's post, or yesterday's?
ASSUNTA. Non c'è posta oggi. Perche non e venuto questa mattina come sempre.
PASQUALE. I could not come this morning. I spent the morning waiting at *Danieli's.* There is an Englishman arriving who wishes for a valet. I cannot live on promises. The money Mr Jessamine sent me has run out.
ASSUNTA. Allora prende il nouvo posto.
PASQUALE. I think I will have to take the new post. But it is not one which pleases me. (*He picks up a wrapped newspaper, moves to L of Assunta, removes the wrapper from the paper and throws it into Assunta's bucket*) What do you suppose can have happened to him? It has been a long time to wait.

(*There is a pause.* ASSUNTA, *having finished the birdcage, bangs it noisily among the other junk*)

(*He moves to the couch LC and sits on the arm*) Was there a parrot here?
ASSUNTA. Si. Un papagallo. Very old, like her mistress.
PASQUALE. How long have you been here, Assunta?
ASSUNTA. Io? No mi ricordo. Circa forse venti cinque anni. Si, si. Venti cinque.
PASQUALE (*incredulously*) A quarter of a century, in this place! (*He sighs*) Was it an educated parrot—could it talk?
ASSUNTA (*rising and picking up the bucket*) Si. E come parlava!
PASQUALE. What did it say?

(ASSUNTA *shrugs, as if to suggest that the parrot could have said anything*)

ASSUNTA (*mockingly*) "La Divina Juliana, La Divina Juliana!"
(*She crosses towards the landing*)

PASQUALE. "*Divina!*" That old bag of bones!

(*The front door bell rings.* ASSUNTA *is in no hurry to answer it and goes on to the landing*)

(*He crosses to Assunta*) Miss Tina is still out? I hoped to see her if I came so late. I never see her. How is she?
ASSUNTA. Sensata e calma. (*She looks out of the landing window. Sharply*) C'è L'Americano! Lo lascio entrare. (*She pulls the front door lever*)
PASQUALE. No, I will go.

(PASQUALE *exits quickly down the stairs* R. *We hear him greet* H.J. *at the bottom of the stairs and then the sound of them coming up.*
H.J. *appears on the landing. He seems to be a changed man. He wears a dark alpaca suit. His face is rather pale*)

ASSUNTA (*cheerfully enough*) Buona sera, Signore.
H.J. Buona sera, Assunta.
ASSUNTA. Spero che stia bene.

(ASSUNTA *exits down the stairs* R. H.J. *pauses on the landing, gazing in sad bewilderment at what has become a storehouse of a room. He looks as Aeneas might have looked revisiting Carthage.* PASQUALE *appears on the landing*)

PASQUALE. Is not the Signora coming in?

H.J. (*crossing to* C) No, Pasquale, the Signora will wait below in the gondola. I am sorry, Pasquale, that I have left you without news of me for so long. How are you?

PASQUALE (*moving* RC) Very happy to see you back, my lord.

H.J. (*moving up* R *of the table; tonelessly*) Yes. (*He moves about, still taking in the scene of desolation around him*) Tell me, Pasquale, how is . . .?

PASQUALE. She is calm. At first many tears.

H.J. Tears, eh? (*He crosses to the stove*) I wrote a letter to Miss Tina to ask news of her actual state, but it is possible that the reply went to the Poste Restante at Treviso when I was at Castelfranco. (*He inspects the stove, then moves up* C *and indicates the double doors*) Where is she now? In there, I suppose?

PASQUALE (*surprised*) No, she is out.

H.J. (*amazed*) Out!

PASQUALE. So Assunta has said.

H.J. (*coming to life and moving above the table towards the windows*) Out! In the garden, I suppose? Is Miss Tina with her? How is Miss Tina? (*He has moved towards the windows as if to look down into the garden, but his eye is caught by his letters which are resting on a pile of junk on the table. He picks up a letter and starts to open it*)

PASQUALE (*puzzled*) As I say, she is calm now. At first, many people, dottori, avvocati. But since the funeral she is sensible and calm.

H.J. (*looking at Pasquale in horror*) The funeral? Miss Bordereau's funeral?

PASQUALE. But yes, Signore. They have put her into the earth, quella vecchia.

H.J. She's dead?

PASQUALE. So it appears, since they have buried her.

(H.J. *crosses to the door down* R, *tries the handle but finds it locked*)

H.J. When was the funeral?

PASQUALE. It was a week after you have left. (*He moves up* L *of the couch* RC) But a funeral you could scarcely call it, Signore. Two gondolas, poor thing. And two old ladies and an old gentleman came in a gondola of their own and supported Miss Tina to Murano.

H.J. (*moving to the left end of the couch* RC *and sitting*) Murano! Then they were Catholics! To think I hadn't even discovered that.

PASQUALE. And then, Signore, I was there. I did what a man could.

(H.J. *tries for a moment or two to take in all the implications of this*)

H.J. Tell me, Pasquale, what happened that night after I left.

PASQUALE. I put the old woman back in her bed. And then— I was starting to pull the trunk back in there when I heard Assunta coming upstairs. I hid it over there. Just in time. For then Miss Tina arrived with the doctor. At first Miss Tina did not ask where you were. She was too worried. When she asked, I said I thought you had gone to find another doctor.

H.J. And next morning?

PASQUALE. Next morning I said you had received a telegram and had had to leave the house early. That you did not wish to disturb. You had hoped the old woman was better. You see, I did not let you down, my lord, I did what a man could.

H.J. I am sure you did, Pasquale. Thank you.

PASQUALE. Don't mench. (*He crosses to the landing*)

H.J. But what did she say when I did not return?

PASQUALE (*moving to R of the couch* RC) I did not see her for two whole days. She never left the bedside. When I had your letter from Castelfranco I said you were staying there. On business.

(H.J. *rises, crosses to* C *then turns to Pasquale*)

H.J. Then she knows nothing? Where is she now? Do you know?

PASQUALE. She left the house very early for Mass, as usual, but Assunta says she is often out now she is alone.

H.J. And about time, too. Pasquale, go and ask the Signora in the gondola please to come in for a minute. Then you can go upstairs and start to get my things together.

PASQUALE. Yes, my lord.

(PASQUALE *goes to the landing and exits down the stairs* R. H.J. *moves towards the double doors. He puts his hands on the handles and, quickly and deliberately, as if expecting a ghost, pulls them open. The rooms beyond are in utter darkness. He turns and looks back at the changed sala. In his mind he is obviously re-living the last moments that he was in the house. There are steps below. H.J. pulls the doors gently to behind him.*

MRS PREST *and* PASQUALE *enter up the stairs* R. MRS PREST *is dressed in some fashionable outfit, autumnal, but brilliant. H.J. moves up* R *of the table.*

PASQUALE, *when he has escorted Mrs Prest to the top of the stairs, discreetly retires up the stairs* R. *When he has gone, H.J. speaks*)

H.J. She is dead.

MRS PREST. Yes, I know. Pasquale has just told me. (*She crosses to* R *of H.J. After a pause*) Why didn't you tell me at the time instead of running off like that? I might have been able to help you.

H.J. Helen, I swear I did not know she was dead. If I had, I would have believed myself a criminal. (*He leans on the trunk on the table*) I just ran out of the house. As I fled down those stairs, I could hear the wings of the furies following me.

MRS PREST. Is there anything you want me to do?

H.J. Advise me. She is out somewhere. It seems she has taken to life again.

MRS PREST. Good.

H.J. That's what I said. (*He toys with the letters on the table*) I don't know whether to wait for her or come back later.

MRS PREST. Are you asking me to give you the signal to go ahead? To take this precious opportunity to steal the papers?

H.J. (*looking sharply at her*) Helen!

MRS PREST. Well, Harry, be honest.

H.J. I mean, would you care to wait with me now, or should we come back, at your convenience, later?

MRS PREST. Harry, why do you always shelter behind my bustle? Come back for what, precisely?

H.J. To see her, of course.

MRS PREST. Why should you not see her by yourself?

H.J. For the reason you have guessed. I am ashamed.

(*The shutter clacks sharply.* MRS PREST *crosses above H.J. towards the shutters and then to* L *of him*)

MRS PREST (*after a pause*) There is something you have not told me yet.

H.J. *She* trusted me. She trusted even my lies.

MRS PREST. Then I was wrong. I was beginning to think she was not lacking in feminine guile. But I was wrong. She is a fool.

(*There is a pause. There is a distant flash of lightning and the shutter clacks again twice*)

H.J. Look! If I stay, with or without you, I give you my solemn word I have no intention of stealing one single page even if I knew where to lay my hands on it. I never had any such intention. That you must believe.

MRS PREST (*looking at him*) I believe you.

(*There is a roll of distant thunder.* MRS PREST *glances towards the windows. The shutter clacks again*)

But I am not sure the Gods do. That's thunder. They are growling at you. (*She moves to the windows and looks out at the garden*)

(H.J. *reads one of his letters*)

MRS PREST. So this is the famous garden. The innocent excuse for all the trouble.

(TINA *enters up the stairs* R, *unseen by the others. She is dressed in*

*a ready-made mourning dress which, although not well made, gives her
an air of smartness, compared to the clothes in which we had previously
seen her. She wears a bonnet and is carrying a small bunch of red roses
which she has bought at a flower stall. She stands on the landing
looking at them both)*

H.J. *She* will believe me. Miss Tina will believe me. She has
a good soul and she can trust.

(Mrs Prest, *turning to look at H.J. sees Tina and crosses towards
her)*

Mrs Prest. My dear! I am Helen Prest.

(H.J. *wheels round and sees Tina)*

I don't suppose you will remember me. I am very glad to see you
looking so well. What a terrible time you must have had. I made
Harry bring me along today to say how deeply sorry I am. If
only I had known . . .
Tina. Yes, I do remember you. You are very kind.
Mrs Prest. Did you have anyone to help you?
Tina. Oh, yes. When the "nice" Italians like you, they like
you for life.

(H.J. *stands there dumb.* Mrs Prest *looks at H.J. and then at
Tina, sensing the situation)*

Mrs Prest *(sociably)* Would you think it very rude of me if I
invited myself to look at the garden that I have heard so much
about?

(Tina *vaguely shakes her head and moves into the room)*

(She arrests Tina with a gesture) No, please don't bother to show me,
I will find the way. Gardens are best when you come on them by
surprise. *(She turns to go to the windows)*
Tina. I think there is going to be a storm.
Mrs Prest *(stopping and turning)* Let us hope so, we need one.
Yesterday's just huffed its way round the lagoon and went back
to sea again. *(She moves towards the windows)* Harry, you will wait
for me, won't you?

(Mrs Prest *exits on to the balcony)*

(Off) Oh, it's charming, charming!
H.J. *(moving up* LC*)* I cannot let my friend say everything for
me. I am most deeply grieved to hear of your bereavement.
Tina. Yes. *(She pauses)* Thank you.
H.J. I expect you were beginning to wonder what had hap-
pened to me.
Tina. Yes.
H.J. I hope you didn't think that I would never come back?

TINA (*with a step further into the room*) Yes.

H.J. You mean you did think that? But Pasquale gave you my message?

TINA. Oh, yes.

H.J. Your aunt—the end came some days after I left?

TINA (*moving above the couch* RC) Yes. Two days.

H.J. I wish I had known. The funeral must have been last Tuesday?

(TINA *nods*)

Was she in pain?

TINA. No.

H.J. Thank God!

(TINA *puts her flowers and handbag on the couch* RC *and removes her bonnet*)

TINA. At first when she came to and opened her eyes there was no life in them, no sense. But then she fell into a long sleep. The next day she opened her eyes again and I spoke to her. She didn't answer but she looked at me. I know she saw and understood. Her eyes were more wonderful than ever. Then she went to sleep again. We don't know exactly when she went to sleep for good. (*She puts her bonnet on the couch* RC)

H.J. I curse myself for not being here. Why did you not let me know? And you managed everything by yourself? You have been very brave.

TINA (*removing her gloves*) Oh, I could never have managed anything by myself. But there is always someone, I suppose. (*She puts her gloves with her bag*) The Good Sisters told some of our old friends. They arranged things and came with me to the Island cemetery. I think it must be beautiful to be buried there. You know, I was surprised with myself. I cried a great deal at first, I just couldn't help it. (*She moves to* R *of the couch* RC) But I didn't feel the way I expected to. I suppose it was because she had so often talked about it. Ever since I can remember she was always saying: "Where would you be without me?" (*She comes to a stop*)

(H.J. *deliberately does not ask her the obvious question*)

H.J. (*moving* C) I wish I had been here to help you.

TINA (*moving below the couch* RC) Perhaps we could have helped each other.

H.J. (*curiously*) How do you mean?

TINA. I thought at first you had gone for some little journey. I remember thinking how nice it must be to be free to make some little *giro* whenever one wants to. (*She sits on the left end of the couch* RC) Pasquale told me, when he had your letter, that you would soon return.

H.J. (*moving down* LC) I intended to, but somehow the days

passed. I jogged along in the carriage, I saw that magnificent Giorgione at Castelfranco. I hung about in the golden air. Much as I love Venice, it is sometimes good, especially in summer, to get away from it.

TINA. Oh, how I would like to get away from it.

H.J. (*cautiously*) That could not be arranged?

TINA. Oh, yes, yes, it could, now. For you see, thanks to you there is some money in the house.

H.J. (*with a step towards her*) I am delighted to hear it. And have you thought of what you are going to do? Have you some general plan?

TINA (*brightly*) Oh, yes, oh, yes. But I haven't settled anything yet. I didn't like to go without . . . (*She breaks off*)

(H.J. *looks sharply at Tina and turns away*)

H.J. (*hurriedly*) Of course I realize that you are not expecting me to stay on as a lodger. About this house—what is your tenure here? What have you on your hands in the way of a lease?

TINA (*closing up slightly*) The house is ours. Mine. It was bought, so the avvocato tells me, years ago.

H.J. That is good news. It will assure you an income.

TINA. Yes, but this quarter is not fashionable any more. The avvocato tells me I must not expect much.

H.J. (*gaining confidence and moving to the french windows*) I think I must meet this avvocato. I would not like to think of a bad lawyer settling anyone's fate. (*He turns and moves above the table*) And talking of fate—it makes me very nervous to say this—what of mine?

TINA. Your fate? (*She suddenly loses any confidence she had*)

H.J. (*moving* C) I mean about our papers. Are there any? You must know now.

TINA (*in considerable agitation; her voice trembling*) There were a great many. More than I supposed.

H.J. (*gesturing to the doors up* C; *scarcely less agitated*) Do you mean that they are in there and that I may see them?

TINA. They are not in there and I am afraid you can't see them.

H.J. (*with a step towards her*) You don't mean to say you made her a death-bed promise? It was precisely against your doing anything of that sort that I thought I was safe.

TINA. No, I gave no promise.

H.J. Well, then?

TINA. She tried to burn them. She had dragged them all the way out here to the big stove. I can't understand how she did it, because Assunta didn't help her. She tells me so and I believe her. I found it there after I had got back with the doctor. The doctor thinks that's what brought on her attack.

H.J. (*moving down* LC; *controlling his fears*) Why should she have done that in the middle of the night?

TINA (*hesitantly*) Night and day were all the same to her.

H.J. (*moving to her; bold in his fears*) I hope you don't think it was because of me?

(TINA *looks at him*)

I mean, she didn't believe that I was here to steal them?

TINA (*whispering shamefacedly*) I am afraid I did think that at first. But Assunta says Pasquale was here with you. I could hardly believe that you had gone into her room and brought the trunk in here.

H.J. (*sincerely*) No, whatever I may have been tempted to do, I could not have done that.

TINA. Then she must have brought it in here herself. After all, Pasquale knew nothing bout Mr Aspern's papers, surely?

H.J. (*moving above the couch* RC; *with firm emphasis*) No, I give you my word, Pasquale knew nothing about Mr Aspern's papers. They would have no interest for Pasquale.

TINA. No, no, of course not.

(H.J.'s *eye alights on the curious pile of rugs by the door down* R. *He longs to look and see whether the green trunk is not just there, but he refrains*)

H.J. (*moving down* R *of the couch* RC) You told me once, do you remember, that you would help me.

TINA. I said: "I will help you if I can."

H.J. Well, then, Miss Tina . . . (*He sits* R *of Tina on the couch* RC)

TINA. You see, she told me—she charged me—oh, it was terrible.

H.J. I thought you said she never spoke after that night?

TINA. No, she couldn't, after that night. And even then . . . But she could make signs.

H.J. Did you tell her you'd burn them?

TINA. No—I didn't—on purpose.

H.J. (*holding Tina by the arms*) On purpose? For me?

TINA. Yes, only for that. (*She rises, crosses to* R *of the table* LC, *and leans against it*)

H.J. But what good will it do me if after all you feel that you can't show them to me?

TINA (*dismally*) Oh, none—I know that—I know that. But I can't.

H.J. Do you think she believed that you had destroyed them?

TINA. I don't know what she believed at the last. I couldn't tell, she was too far gone.

H.J. (*rising and moving to* R *of Tina*) Then if there was no promise and no assurance I can't see what ties you.

TINA. Oh, she hated it so—she hated it so—she was so jealous.

(H.J. *moves up* LC *and faces up stage, exasperated. He turns and again looks at what he supposes to be the fateful trunk on the floor down* R. TINA *moves to the couch* LC, *partially removes the dust sheet and takes from under it the portrait which Juliana had offered to H.J. By removing the dust sheet she discloses the true whereabouts of the green trunk.* H.J. *does not immediately see this*)

Here is the portrait that interested you. You may have that.

H.J. (*moving to* R *of Tina*) Do you mean—you give it to me?

TINA. I give it to you. (*She hands the portrait to H.J. and crosses below him to* RC)

H.J. (*not daring to look at the portrait*) But it is worth money, a large sum.

TINA. Well?

H.J. (*turning to her*) More than I told her. If all this could come to light, half a dozen museums in America would outbid each other for this.

TINA. Good!

H.J. I can't take it from you as a gift. I would like to possess it, but I can't pay you for it, according to the idea Miss Bordereau had of its value.

TINA. Well then, sell it to one of those museums.

H.J. God forbid! I prefer the picture to the money.

TINA. Well, then, keep it.

H.J. (*after a pause*) You're very generous.

TINA. So are you.

H.J. (*cautiously*) I don't know why you should think so.

TINA. Well, you've made a great difference to me.

(H.J. *becomes embarrassed, moves away* L *and turns his attention to the portrait.* TINA *moves and sits on the left end of the couch* RC)

H.J. (*studying the portrait*) Look at those eyes. So young and brilliant, yet so wise and deep. He is smiling—perhaps even laughing at me. I seem to have got us all into a pretty pickle for him. (*At this moment he sees the trunk. He turns and looks at Tina*) Is this a bribe?

(TINA *looks puzzled*)

(*He crosses to* C *and faces her. Almost harshly*) Are you bribing me—to give up the papers? Much as I value this, you know, if I were obliged to choose, the papers are what I would prefer.

(TINA, *a little outraged, a little frightened by his tone, rises and moves to* R *of H.J.*)

TINA (*slowly*) How can you choose? How can you choose?

H.J. Of course, if that's how you see it. To part with them seems to you impiety, sacrilege?

TINA (*shaking her head queerly*) You'd understand if you'd really known her. I was afraid. (*She moves up* c) She was terrible when she was angry.

H.J. (*moving to her*) Yes, I saw something of that that night. Her eyes blazed.

TINA. They stare at me in the dark.

(TINA *turns to H.J. There is a nearer flash of lightning.* TINA *winces and covers her face with her hands.* H.J. *takes her in his arms as she buries her head in his shoulder*)

H.J. You've grown nervous with all you've been through. (*He puts a protective arm around her shoulders*)

TINA. Oh yes, very. (*She seems content to stay within the protection of his arm*)

(H.J. *does not withdraw his arm but his gaze turns towards the green trunk. He does not fully realize his power over Tina but at this moment he senses it enough to make a high bid. He releases her*)

H.J. You mustn't let me stand here as if it were in my soul to tempt you to—do anything base. Naturally, I give up my rooms. I leave Venice immediately.

TINA (*withdrawing slightly and gazing at him*) Immediately! Do you mean today?

H.J. (*amazed at the desolation in her voice*) Oh, no. Not so long as I can be of the least service to you.

TINA. Well, just a day or two more—just two or three days. (*She controls herself, moves to* R *of the couch* LC *and faces the trunk*) She wanted to say something else to me—the last day—something very particular. But she couldn't.

H.J. Something very particular?

TINA. Something more about the papers.

H.J. (*moving down* c) And did you guess? Have you any idea?

TINA. No. I tried to think—but I didn't know. I've thought all kinds of things.

H.J. As for instance?

TINA (*turning to him; hesitantly*) Well, that if you were a relation it would be different.

H.J. (*moving to her*) If I were a relation?

TINA. If you weren't a stranger—(*she is in the utmost confusion*) then it would be the same for you as for me. Anything that's mine would be yours, you could do what you like. I shouldn't be able to prevent you and you'd have no responsibility.

(H.J. *looks at Tina for a moment or two, and then looks at the portrait in his hand. There is a long and vivid flash of lightning*)

H.J. Yes, I'll sell this for you.

TINA. We can divide the money.

H.J. No, no. It shall be all yours. I think I know what your poor aunt wanted to say. She wanted that the papers should be buried with her.

(TINA *ponders a moment or two before speaking*)

TINA. Oh, no, she wouldn't have thought that safe.

H.J. It seems to me nothing could be safer.

TINA. She had an idea that when people want to publish, they're capable . . .

(TINA *breaks off, blushing, as she sees H.J.'s horrified amazement*)

H.J. Of violating a tomb? Mercy on us! What must she have thought of me?

TINA. She wasn't just. She wasn't generous.

(*There is a roll of thunder, somewhat closer*)

But she was truly fond of me. She wanted me to be happy and if any person should be kind to me—yes, that was what she wanted—to speak of . . . She didn't care for you but she was always thinking of me. She knew I should like it if you could carry out your idea. You could have seen the things—you could have used them.

H.J. You mean . . .?

TINA. Yes, if . . .

(*There is a vivid flash of lightning.* TINA *breaks off as she sees H.J.'s face, which is full of embarrassment, though not without compassion*)

(*She turns away from him in anguish. Vehemently*) I don't know what to do. I'm too tormented; I'm too ashamed. (*She bursts into a flood of tears, then desperately pulls herself together for a second or two*) I'd have given you everything and she'd understand, where she is—she'd forgive me.

H.J. Ah! My dear Miss Tina——

(TINA *looks at him*)

—it wouldn't do. It wouldn't do.

(TINA *does not answer but turns away her head*)

(*He moves up* R, *places the portrait on the table up* RC, *then goes on to the landing*) I must—see how Pasquale is getting on with my packing.

(H.J. *exits up the stairs. There is a brief pause.*
MRS PREST *enters hurriedly and with little squeals of excitement, from the garden. At the sound of her coming* TINA *crosses to the couch* RC *and takes a handkerchief from her handbag*)

MRS PREST. My, that was pretty! (*She crosses to* C)

(TINA *sits on the right end of the couch* RC, *facing* R)

The lagoon looks like lead and then the lightning turns it to silver. The storm has passed us by. Not a drop of rain, but it's cooler, quite a breeze. Where is Harry? Where is Mr Jessamine?

TINA. Mr Jarvis has gone upstairs.

MRS PREST (*putting on her gloves*) He is a strange fellow, don't you think? I suppose you've got to know him quite well during all these months.

TINA. I thought I had.

MRS PREST (*significantly*) Ah, that's just it. How clever of you. It took me three years of what I believed was quite an intimate friendship to realize that at moments I did not know him at all. That's very often the case with literary or artistic people, I think. It is as if one half of them were—mortgaged. (*She stops abruptly, looks searchingly at Tina, then crosses and sits* L *of her on the couch* RC) Oh, my dear, I can't help feeling you are terribly distressed and I feel a fool chattering on like this. Are you sure there is nothing I can do?

TINA. No. You are very kind. I have never been very good at understanding people's little ways. My aunt always said I was a fool.

MRS PREST. Because you were not like the rest of us? Because you don't try to be all things to all people? How many of us would like to be as you are, to be, as the French say, "*sans courbe*". That is a quality as fine as it is rare. Now, you see, Harry has none of that. He is all subtlety, all curves.

(TINA *rises, moves above the couch* RC, *picks up her bunch of flowers and hands them to Mrs Prest*)

TINA. Please take these.

MRS PREST. Oh, thank you. Are they from the garden?

TINA. No. The garden is dried up. The rain—when it comes—will do it good. I bought them. I've come to need flowers again.

MRS PREST (*after a small pause*) Thank you, my dear. I hope Harry won't be all night. I am dining out and I hate dressing in a hurry. (*She glances at her watch*) Oh, goodness! (*She rises and crosses to* C) I know what I'll do. I'll take Harry's gondola as far as the Grand Canal and get another one there. Then his can be back in a matter of minutes. Will you tell him for me, please?

(TINA *nods gravely and moves down* RC)

TINA. Yes.

MRS PREST (*turning to face Tina*) I really must fly. Thanks for the flowers. If there is anything I can do, please count on me, won't you? I shall be at *Danieli's* all this week and I have all the time in the world. (*She crosses to the landing*)

TINA (*with a step towards Mrs Prest; quietly*) Did you say you'd known Mr Jarvis for three years?

(MRS PREST *stops and turns. She watches Tina carefully during the following speech*)

MRS PREST. Oh, bless you, much longer than that. More years than I care to remember. He was wonderfully good-looking, then. (*She moves to* R *of Tina*) Oh, yes, I've watched several heart-breaks—several, and there must have been some that I didn't see. He's been seriously in love twice, I think, though he's never told me a word. Both married women, both beautiful, and, I suppose, clever in a wordly sort of way. It's never ceased to puzzle me what Harry, who has so much that is delicate and spiritual, could ever have seen in them. I don't mean that he is heartless. There are times when he is the best friend, the most charming companion a woman ever had. And then there are times when he is, quite simply, a monster. But there it is. Harry is a paradox.

(TINA *has a faraway look and something of a smile on her face*)

But why on earth am I telling you all this?
TINA. I don't know.
MRS PREST. No more do I. Good-bye, my dear Miss Bordereau. And remember: any time you need me . . .

(MRS PREST *turns and exits quickly down the stairs.*
PASQUALE *enters down the stairs, carrying a suitcase*)

TINA. Pasquale, go and help the lady into the gondola. Take my umbrella in case it rains. (*She indicates her umbrella by the table on the landing*)

(PASQUALE *picks up the umbrella and exits down the stairs* R. *The breeze is getting louder. The shutter clacks.* TINA *crosses to the french windows, firmly closes the shutter then crosses to* C.
H.J. *enters down the stairs, looks out of the landing window then turns to* Tina)

H.J. I am afraid it is too late for me to pack this evening.
TINA. Your friend has gone. If you hurry you could still catch her.
H.J. (*moving* RC) I don't seem to be able to pull myself together.
TINA. Good-bye. I hope you will be happy.
H.J. (*moving to* R *of her*) Good-bye?
TINA. Aren't you going today? But it doesn't matter, for whenever you go I shan't see you again. I don't want to.
H.J. Let me come back tomorrow—to settle things. You know, perhaps tomorrow will show us both everything in a much truer light.
TINA. I don't think it will.
H.J. Then the next day—next week . . .

TINA. Not the next week or next year or even the years to come can alter things as they are.

H.J. My dear Miss Tina, the whole of life teaches us that the moment is never precisely what it seems. It is only later, often much later, that we come to understand the moment.

TINA. I think with me it is the other way round. If I don't understand something at once, I don't understand it at all. I am not clever enough.

H.J. Let us be sure this really is the end of the chapter: there may be several endings.

TINA. But surely only one ending will be the right one?

H.J. Precisely. Let us be sure what it is.

TINA. I know what it is.

H.J. What?

TINA (*smiling in her dejection*) I shall never see you again.

H.J. I would wager anything you like to name that that is not nearly the right ending.

TINA. Would you?

H.J. Yes, anything.

TINA. Would you have wagered your precious papers?

H.J. How do you mean? They are already at stake.

TINA. No.

H.J. How do you mean?

TINA (*after a pause*) They might have been at stake—but I burnt them.

H.J. (*pointing to the green trunk*) But you said just now that I could see them if—if . . .

(TINA *does not immediately answer. It is as if she were daring H.J. to complete the unfinished sentence. When she speaks her voice is almost stern*)

TINA. No, I didn't say that. I said "you could have seen them".

(H.J. *stares at her in horrified disbelief, but the look on* TINA'S *face and the tone of her voice carry conviction.* H.J. *hesitates then crosses below Tina to the green trunk, almost shambling. He throws aside the dust sheet*)

It is empty. I burnt them. (*She picks up her handbag and takes out a key*)

(H.J. *turns to Tina*)

(*She holds out the key*) If you don't believe me . . .

(H.J. *takes the key, turns to the trunk, puts the key in the lock, then hesitates and turns to her*)

(*Her face is impassive*) Why don't you believe me? (*She turns away below the couch* RC *as if dismissing him. From now to the end of the scene, she does not look at H.J.*)

(H.J. *stares at Tina*)

You said once that I was not capable of deceit.

(H.J. *crosses slowly to* L *of Tina*)

H.J. Forgive me. Please forgive me. I shall never cease to reproach myself—for my loss.
TINA. For what loss?
H.J. The loss of my precious papers.
TINA. The storm is passing. I think you must go now.

(H.J. *turns away, goes to the landing and exits down the stairs.* TINA *stands still, and listens for the sound of the front door, or perhaps for his footsteps returning.*

ASSUNTA *enters up the stairs* R *and stops on the landing*)

(*She wheels round to Assunta*) Has he ˜one?
ASSUNTA. Yes, they have all gone. (*She moves to* R *of the couch* RC)

(TINA *crosses to* RC)

You have had nothing to eat all day. What shall I prepare? (*She takes H.J.'s gold match-case from her pocket and crosses to* R *of Tina*) Oh, I found this over there this morning. I think it is his. Maybe I shout after him?
TINA. No, Assunta, give it to me.

(ASSUNTA *hands the match-case to Tina, crosses to the french windows and looks out.* TINA *looks at the match-case. A gust of cold wind blows through the room*)

ASSUNTA. It is cooler now.
TINA. Yes. In fact, it's suddenly rather cold. (*She shivers*) Assunta, I think we'll light the stove. (*She moves to the trunk and unlocks it*) Bring some sticks, will you?
ASSUNTA (*crossing to the landing*) You are cold because you do not eat. Si, signorina, I'll bring sticks and paper.
TINA. No, just bring sticks. I have plenty of paper.

ASSUNTA *exits down the stairs* R. TINA *stands for a moment or two, then opens the trunk, looks inside for a second, then takes out an old battered shako which she lays aside. Then she lifts out the tray of the trunk and carries it to the stove where she puts it on the floor. She lifts out of it a pair of moth-eaten uniform trousers with broad braid down the side. Under the trousers are papers. Packets of them tied in faded ribbons.* TINA *kneels, unties a ribbon and opens out the first piece of paper. She glances at it and reads a few words, then turns it over and looks for a signature. She puts it down, still looking at it as she lights a match from H.J.'s gold match-box. Then she lights the first paper and watches it burn in her hands. When it is thoroughly alight she puts it in the stove. She picks up another letter. As she does so the leaves of the magnolia and the vine on the balcony are shaking in the breeze and a few withered vine-leaves are blown desolately across the floor of the sala. The bells of the nearby churches are chiming, but seem muffled by the cool wind as—*

the CURTAIN *falls*

FURNITURE AND PROPERTY LIST

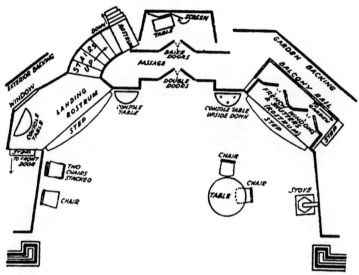

ACT I

On stage—5 upright chairs
    Circular table
    3 console tables
    Gilt screen
    Gilt-top table
    Stove
    Lever and chain
    Door bell

Shutters closed
Doors closed
Landing window closed
Stove out
Stove door open

Off stage—Brass tray. *On it:* plate, bowl covered with muslin (ASSUNTA)
    Wheel chair with cushions and tapestry shawls (JULIANA)

Personal—MRS PREST: gloves, parasol, gold fob watch, handbag. *In it:* visiting-
    card
    H.J.: top hat, walking-stick, gloves, visiting-card, gold watch and
    fob, large silk handkerchief, wallet with letter
    JULIANA: dark silk eye shade

ACT II
SCENE 1

Strike—1 chair
   Tray with bowl, etc.
Set console table upright up LC
Move table LC to RC

Set—3 chairs R, L and above table RC
    Sociable couch LC
    On table RC: red chenille cloth, vase of roses, several letters and news-
        papers by post
    Pedestal table (*down* R *above door*) *On it:* vase of roses
    Pedestal (*up* L *by pillar*) *On it:* vase of roses
    Chair (*by pillar* L)
    On table up LC: vase of mixed flowers
    On table up RC: vase of mixed flowers
    On balcony: potted plant in vase
    Blooms on magnolia in garden
French windows and shutters open
Landing window closed
Double doors closed
Stove out

Off stage—H.J.'s tail suit (PASQUALE)
    Wheel chair (JULIANA)
    Large sun umbrella (ASSUNTA)
    Tray. *On it:* jug of water, glass (PASQUALE)
    Tray. *On it:* tea pot, milk jug, 2 cups, 2 saucers, 2 tea spoons
        (ASSUNTA)

Personal—PASQUALE: nail file
    H.J.: silk handkerchief, hat, stick, gloves, chemist's phial. *In it:* sal
        volatile, notebook and pencil

SCENE 2

Strike—Sociable couch
    All flowers
    All vases except vase on table RC
    Console table down R
    H.J.'s hat, gloves and stick
    Letters, newspapers, tray, phial, etc., from table RC

Set—Battered Victorian couch (LC) *On it:* antimacassars, dust sheet, feather
                          duster, hand brush, Tina's shawl, Tina's
                          handbag with handkerchief
    Bundle of rugs (*down* L *in front of stove*)
    Leather four-fold screen behind couch
Move pedestal from up L to below left end of screen. *On it:* oil lamp
Move chair C to below table RC

Double doors closed
French windows and shutters open
Landing window closed
Stove out

Off stage—2 rugs, carpet beater (ASSUNTA)
    Portrait in black velvet bag (JULIANA)
    2 sheets (ASSUNTA)
    Gold match-case (PASQUALE)

Personal—TINA: ring
    H.J.: notebook and pencil

SCENE 3

Strike—All rugs from bundle from L, except the top one

Set—*Down* L *in place of rugs:* green trunk with fastenings facing stove, and
    covered with top rug and dust sheet so that the trunk completely
    resembles the bundle in the previous scene
    Under right end of couch: Juliana's eye shade
    Behind screen: wheel chair with shawl
    On landing table: oil lamp

Double doors closed
French windows open
Shutters closed
Lamps lit
Landing window closed
Off stage—Hand oil lamp (H.J.)
      Bunch of violets (TINA)
Personal—H.J.: cigar, gold match-case, watch, notebook and pencil, handkerchief
      TINA: handbag. *In it:* handkerchief

ACT III

Set—Down R, *below door:* vase and pile of plates
      Down R, *above door:* bundle of rugs, covered with rug to look like covered trunk. *On it:* tailor's basket dummy, gondolier's hat, napkins. *Beside it:* 5 vases
      Down RC: social couch covered with dust sheet. *On it:* pile of napkins
      Down RC: Victorian parrot cage, wooden bucket, hand brush, duster
      On landing table: 4 oil lamps
      Above landing table: Tina's umbrella
      On table up R: feather duster. *Beside it:* 2 old oil paintings
      Down L, *above stove:* crumpled soft rug, pile of books, pile of plates
      Below french windows: rolled rug
      Down LC: Victorian couch. *On it:* green trunk containing shako, uniform trousers, papers tied with faded ribbons; up-turned console table with pile of books, portrait in velvet bag
      Trunk and velvet bag covered by dust sheet to look like bundle of odds and ends
      L *of couch* LC: up-turned console table
      Above couch LC: leather screen, on its side, leaning against back of couch
      Up R *of couch* LC: circular table. *On it:* large brown trunk, letters and newspapers by post, partly covered by dust sheet
      R *of table:* 2 stacked chairs with pile of books and bronze statue
      L *of table:* pedestal table with up-turned chair and pile of books
      Up L: pedestal, gilt screen, 2 stacked chairs, pile of books
      L *of double doors:* 4 large vases, large garden vase containing parasols, umbrellas and carpet beater
Double doors closed
French windows open
Shutters swinging open in wind
Lamps out
Off stage—Small bunch of red roses (TINA)
      Suitcase (PASQUALE)
      Gold match-case (ASSUNTA)
Personal—TINA: handbag. *In it:* handkerchief, key
      MRS PREST: watch

NOTE

The staircase leading from the street below could come into view *upstage* of the landing, and the stairs leading on to the upper floors could be downstage of the landing. This, it will be evident, is a great saving in the expense of building the set as well as saving a good deal of room at the side of a narrow stage.

Where the play is produced on a very shallow stage it will probably be found advisable to put the central double doors up left and to make the necessary adjustments. The problem of manœuvring a wheel-chair, even on a full-sized stage, is not an easy one.

When the doors are placed centre stage it will probably be found more convenient to let them open downstage. The baize doors are optional.

LIGHTING PLOT

Property Fittings Required—2 oil table lamps, 1 oil hand lamp

Interior. A Venetian "sala". The same scene throughout
THE MAIN ACTING AREAS ARE—down R, up R, C, up C, up L, down L and at a table LC

ACT I   A Spring afternoon

THE APPARENT SOURCES OF LIGHT ARE—french windows up L and two small windows up R

To open: Effect of Mediterranean sunshine dimmed by louvres of window shutters

Cue 1	H.J. opens shutters	(page 11)
	Bring up general lighting	

ACT II   SCENE 1   Afternoon

To open: Effect of afternoon sunshine

Cue 2	At end of Scene	(page 36)
	Dim all lights to BLACK-OUT	

ACT II   SCENE 2   Early evening

To open: Sunset effect

Cue 3	At end of Scene	(page 47)
	Dim all lights to BLACK-OUT	

ACT II   SCENE 3   Night

THE APPARENT SOURCES OF LIGHT ARE—2 oil lamps, one on landing R and one on pedestal L

To open: The stage dimly lit
Moonlight effect through shutters L and landing window
Oil lamp R, lit fully
Oil lamp L, dim

Cue 4	H.J. enters with lamp	(page 47)
	Bring up lights a little R	
Cue 5	TINA turns up lamp L	(page 48)
	Bring up lamp L	
	Bring up covering lights L	
Cue 6	TINA turns down lamp L	(page 49)
	Dim lamp L	
	Reduce covering lights	
Cue 7	H.J. exits with lamp	(page 49)
	Dim lights a little R	
Cue 8	H.J. enters with lamp	(page 50)
	Bring up lights a little R	
Cue 9	TINA turns up lamp L	(page 50)
	Bring up lamp L	
	Bring up covering lights	

ACT III Afternoon

To open: Effect of lowering, stormy daylight

Cue 10   Mrs Prest: "She is a fool."   (page 60)
           Distant flash of lightning

Cue 11   Tina: ". . . in the dark."   (page 66)
           Nearer flash of lightning

Cue 12   Tina: ". . . have no responsibility."   (page 66)
           Long and vivid flash of lightning

Cue 13   Tina: "Yes, if . . ."   (page 67)
           Vivid flash of lightning

EFFECTS PLOT

ACT I

Cue 1   At rise of Curtain   (page 1)
           2 church clocks, overlapping, chime ½ hour

Cue 2   Assunta opens door up c   (page 2)
           Sound of front door bell

Cue 3   Assunta works lever   (page 2)
           Sound of bolts and creaks of front door and lever

Cue 4   H.J.: "I have an idea."   (page 11)
           Front door slams

Cue 5   H.J. exits to garden   (page 11)
           Bells chime ¾ hour

Cue 6   H.J.: "Red?"   (page 17)
           Spring bell rings

ACT II

SCENE 1

No cues

SCENE 2

Cue 7   Tina sits on couch   (page 37)
           Sound of gondolier singing in the distance

SCENE 3

No cues

ACT III

Cue 8   After rise of Curtain   (page 56)
           Distant thunder from time to time during the Act, with wind effect

Cue 9   Pasquale: ". . . bag of bones."   (page 57)
           Front door bell rings

Cue 10   H.J.: "I am ashamed."   (page 60)
           The shutter clacks sharply

Cue 11   Mrs Prest: "She is a fool."   (page 60)
           The shutter clacks twice

THE GREEN HUSSARS

Words by
MICHAEL REDGRAVE

Music by
JAMES BERNARD

But there con-tent I'd be, my bod-y his King—dom,

No foe could fright him there, No wars al - arm - - - -

Where are the Green Hus-sars who left the town smi- - - - - ling

Where are the cheers of that bright sum-mer morn - -?

What cheer is com-fort to a wo-man that's wail — ing

What fel-low fath-ers now my child un - born - - - - - - -?

- - - - - - - - - ?

Verse 2 is optional and was omitted in the original production.

The tune may of course be transposed to whatever key is most comfortable for the singer.